NASHVILLE 1864

NASHVILLE

1864

THE DYING OF THE LIGHT

A NOVEL

MADISON JONES

J. S. SANDERS & COMPANY

NASHVILLE

1997

Published in the United States by:
J. S. Sanders & Company
P.O. Box 50331
Nashville, Tennessee 37205

Library of Congress Cataloging-in-Publication Data

Jones, Madison, 1925–
    Nashville 1864 : a novel / Madison Jones. — 1st ed.
        p.   cm.
    ISBN 1-879941-35-x (alk. paper)
    1. Tennessee—History—Civil War, 1861–1865—Fiction.
    2. Nashville (Tenn.), Battle of, 1864—Fiction.   I. Title.
PS3560.O517N37   1997
813′.54—dc21   96-29800
                                                                      CIP

Design by Christine Taylor
Composition by Wilsted & Taylor Publishing Services

Printed in the United States of America

FIRST EDITION

1 3 5 7 9 10 8 6 4 2

In memory of my grandfather
John Glenn Webber
1856–1944

Do not go gentle into that good night.
Rage, rage against the dying of the light.

DYLAN THOMAS

The following memoir is the work of my paternal grandfather Steven Moore. According to the manuscript, in a hand that is still quite vivid, it was written, or at least completed in 1900. Since he was born in 1852, this puts it in his forty-eighth year, roughly thirty-six years after the Civil War Battle of Nashville which is the memoir's principal focus.

The memoir was pretty well neglected throughout the lifetime of my father Edward Moore who was a great deal more interested in making money in the real estate business than in matters to do with history. All through my boyhood and early manhood it lay practically undisturbed in a trunk in our attic. I remember seeing it there and skimming through with the thought that it looked interesting enough for me to read someday when I had leisure from the pleasures of youth. But this never happened until my father's death when I was in my forties and the disposition of his property put the manuscript in my hands instead of my brother's. By that time I had become a rather serious-minded fellow, a good deal less than pleased with what I saw happening in Nashville and elsewhere, and the reading of this memoir went straight to my heart. It also left me not a little embarrassed, even ashamed, that I could have lived in such blithe indifference to what had been before me, in my own family and in our world. Since then I have read it numerous times, never without responding in much the same way. But it was only recently, here in my old age, that I decided to seek publication for it. My hope is that it may affect others as it surely has affected me.

My grandfather was a well-read man, a lawyer who entered the profession only by his reading of the law. He was also a man of considerable sensibility, as his well-told story may testify. I wish I could remember him better, but he died when I was only six. I do recall him as a person who did not often speak, but who was very gentle and polite and who wore a rather sad expression. More than once I heard my father, not always quite kindly, describe him that way, as given to melancholy. On the basis of his memoir, this condition of mind, or soul, is not surprising.

The memoir portrays in rather sketchy form life as experienced by my grandfather's family, a representative one, throughout most of the war years when Nashville was occupied by the Union army. But the focus is on my grandfather's own personal experience, as a twelve-year-old boy, of the Battle of Nashville, which took place on December 15 and 16 of 1864. I have already mentioned that this is a story well-told, and lest the reader, considering the lapse of so many years, think it too well-told, I have this to say. It is probable that in some small details, like ones of feeling and gesture, he did find it necessary to re-create in imagination. But this is not to falsify. It is only to do what any artist must: make memory come alive to its fullest in the crucible of his art. As for such as material facts and events in their actual sequence, I see no reason here to doubt the writer's perfect integrity.

We live in a time when it has become routine, at least in the most influential quarters, to view the Old South as a veritable nest of evils. This view was already there in its infancy even at the time when my grandfather wrote, and there is good reason to think that some part of his intention here was to counteract it. For me, at least, he quite successfully did so.

CHAPTER ONE

*I*t is probable that most Southerners feel at least a good measure of what I feel about the old days. The passing of thirty-five years is not enough to diminish by very much the pain that always comes, at least to me, in the remembered presence of that devastating time. My case, I believe, is special, though. My circumstances surely played a large part in this specialness, but looking back I can see that much of it had its cause in my own character. I think that there was, or is, too much in me of what was already abundant in Southern people generally: an ideality that almost no facts in a case could mitigate.

Of course in those war years I was a child—nine when it began, nearly thirteen when it ended. Nashville, only a few miles east of our farm on Charlotte Pike, was an occupied city from late February of 1862 on, and this fact alone, the mere presence of the enemy like a constant trumpet in our ears, the more inflamed my already impassioned spirit. I hated the Yankees. I remember thinking, intending, dreaming that on my twelfth birthday, before sun-up, I would steal from my bed, pick up my shotgun and the bundle I had prepared, and set out to join the Army of Tennessee no matter where it was. Join Forrest's cavalry, if he would have me, slash with my saber through the lines of bluebelly Yankee hirelings. Except for the desperate need of my presence there at home I might very likely have tried it.

My father, Jason Moore, joined the Confederate army in '62 just a couple of weeks before our troops retreated through Nashville in the face of the oncoming Yankees. I was only ten at the time but I was already a help around the house and in the garden and in a dozen other ways important on a farm. I was even charged with much of the responsibility of caring for my two baby sisters, and so, more and more, my over-worked mother came to depend on me. Of course we had slave help, one family with two boys and two girls. But the girls were too young to be of any real help and the older boy, Cice, about sixteen in '62, could not be depended on for much. In fact a year or so later he ran away for good. That left Pompey, the father, his always sickly wife Ella, and Dink who was my age and my companion in most things. So what we had was one man, one able woman and two boys to work and maintain more than two hundred acres of farmland, buildings including our rather big house, and livestock, till the Yankees took it all.

Until then, till '64, we had just managed to hobble along. We had suffered depredation, all right, plunder of our livestock, cornfields, garden and smokehouse not only by detachments authorized for the job, but also by strays, mere criminals, Yankee soldiers and otherwise. In '63 the better two of our three teams of mules were confiscated and we were left to make out as best we could with a team half crippled by age. There was also the constant feeling of threat, nights when my mother with a loaded shotgun would come out of her bedroom and settle down in the dark at the head of the stairs, watching, listening. One night she fired it, a noise as stunning as a cannon shot just outside my room. She said there had been somebody on the porch trying the front hall door. Nothing else happened, though, the silence after went unbroken. The next morning we had to cover with tow cloth the ragged gap where the window light had been.

As this event may indicate, my mother, Amantha, was a strong woman—strong in the way that I recall as being characteristic of Southern women in those days. Not that she ruled in our family. There was a line she would not cross, or would cross only in rare moments of stress, that was my father's domain where the final word resided. But her domain was large and scrupulously respected by him. Even allowing for the distortions that time can impose on memory, I am sure that it was as harmonious a marriage as fortune has ever permitted me to witness. I recall especially the manner in which they regularly spoke to each other on subjects of any importance: exactly as though in the matter at hand the other one was the true authority.

I have in my memory many vivid pictures of my mother and father, together and separately. But none is more clearly fixed there than the one from that late spring day in '62 just as Father was preparing to set out for the army. All of us were present, white and black, in front of the stable door, half-circled around the horse whose reins my mother instead of Pompey was holding. The horse's name was Windward, a handsome claybank gelding that my father had not included among the horses he had earlier donated to the Confederate army. Windward stood saddled and ready, a sheathed rifle in front of the stirrup on his off-side and a pack behind on his cruppers. In my memory Father, like the rest of us, including the horse, abides there frozen out of time, he by much the taller looking gravely down into my mother's face. No movement, no sound. I suspect it may not have been just so in those moments, but always when that picture comes back into my mind it is fused with a kind of despairing sadness engendered by an ancient folk ballad my mother used to sing sometimes. It contained these lines:

> *All saddled and bridled and gallant to see.*
> *Home came his good horse*
> *But never came he.*

I have never since heard that ballad, or read it in a book, that I did not shed a few secret tears.

It was only a single day before Father's departure that his intention was actually voiced in my presence, though the signs of it had been visible to me for a week and more. In those last days he had ceased to be the man of few words I had always known. I would overhear him delivering to Mother or to Pompey detailed and lengthy instructions that would have appeared absurdly unnecessary if I had not already guessed what was about to happen. There was his busyness about small repairs to the house and fences, and his trips by wagon into town for household stores in quantities that in the past would have been deemed excessive. And there was his gentleness, beyond the usual, to Mother, to my little sisters and, in his fashion, to me. Then, on that final day, he spoke to me directly.

Weather in Middle Tennessee is changeable in winter. Suddenly, in the wake of days of bitter rain and sleet, there will come an air like balm on cheek and forehead, a spell like high springtime when men and women shed their coats and children their shoes without discomfort—intervals made half-dreamlike in the slanting rays of the sun. Such was that last day, when Father and I stood side by side with our hands on the rail fence in front of the house, looking down toward the pike and the creek bottom beyond. Breaking a full minute of silence, he said,

"You know, Steven, that I leave early tomorrow."

I think I nodded.

"I have no choice any longer. I had hoped . . . I don't know what I hoped. I didn't want this war. But we have it, and they are coming . . . so very many of them. They are not even far away any longer. I'm afraid they will take Nashville."

"But General Johnston'll stop them . . . Won't he?" I said, looking up, up into his bearded face and eyes cold blue in the sunlight.

"It's been badly handled. Our preparation was slow in coming, and clumsy. The fault of too much pride, I'm afraid, in our own strength and valor."

"But won't Johnston keep them from crossing the river?" I said, now finding it hard to speak. "Can't he hold them back, from our side of the river? With cannons and all?"

"That is what people say. I doubt it. I don't think he has the power, not at present. They may cross the river in pursuit of our army, but I don't think they'll pass this way. Straight through Nashville, or farther east, I expect. But we can't be sure. I have given your mother instructions. I wish I had a choice but I don't. Even if I played the coward and stayed here, I would surely be taken prisoner."

Bursting out with it I said, "They couldn't do that to you!" They could not, not to my father, tall and strong and brave as he was. And gallant. In that moment, as I had done before in these last days, I envisioned a bright scarlet plume in the big gray hat he wore.

"War's like that, Steven. That's what happens. That and death and destruction. You will have to take the place of a man, Steven, whatever happens. I have good hopes that, if they do come this way, they will behave like civilized people. I pray they will."

My gaze shifted away from his face, down to where his intent blue eyes seemed fixed. It was the pike at the foot of the long slope, of red clay made redder still by all the recent rain. Then, in my imagination, there at a distance up the pike where it curved from behind the hill was a blue column of Yankee soldiers silently coming on. The vision held for a second, and was gone. But it might be real, might come to be so. Then all this, this house behind us, beautiful with its two white columns and balcony overhead, stable and barn and Pompey's cabin, the rich bottom field stretching out beyond the pike for half a mile to the creek, would not be ours anymore. It was a thought that for a few moments eclipsed even my father's voice. He was speaking about Mother and my little sisters, as if committing them solely to my care. Then, after a pause, he said,

"I'm confident you can depend on Pompey. He was brought here as an infant and I'm sure he expects to die here. About Cice, I don't know. Keep your eye on him."

This was the end of that conversation. Unless you

could call the minute or two that followed, in which my father did something he had never done before, a silent extension of it. He put his hand and held it there on top of mine on the fence rail. I thought of it as the laying on of my commission, the moment of my resolve to act, as far as I was able at ten years old, the part of a grown man. Even the thought was a heavy burden.

Father was right about the immediate future. General Johnston found that he could not hold at Bowling Green with only fifteen thousand troops and so retreated south and crossed the river at Nashville. But Nashville too was found to be not defendable and the army continued its retreat, on south and west across the Tennessee River. Almost the next day, as I remember, the Yankees crossed the Cumberland and occupied Nashville. Immediately they gave evidence of intending to stay there. Within days they began fortifying their new and strategically valuable possession. From our distance of a few miles we witnessed this with alarm. It was like having the ground, our ground, violently snatched from under our feet.

But it was some time before we began to feel the material consequences of the occupation. For a couple of months the only visible evidence of Yankee presence was half a dozen detachments of soldiers in blue uniforms, usually mounted, passing by on the pike. None of them ever stopped, but from our places of concealment, which we sought when they came into view, we could see their upturned faces and sometimes a raised hand pointing. Laying plans, we would think, and afterwards go uneasy about our business.

Full springtime had blossomed before we suffered our first actual visit from Yankees. Father had given my mother many detailed instructions, which she scrupulously followed. Among the more important were those concerning our livestock. A good part of our acreage was spread over the hills behind the house, in part wooded, making it possible, up to a point, to hide our mules and cattle. So we did, successfully for a while, making good use of the clever detail which Mother herself had added on: that of leaving the old, decrepit team of mules in the stable lot and declaring to the Yankees that the other teams had been seized by the Confederate army. In extension of this stratagem we plowed and planted only a few acres in the creek bottom across the pike and actually planted most of our corn crop on the back side of two hills where pasture had been before. There was no such way to protect the chickens and pigs. The best we could do was turn them out of their pens, letting them go more or less wild and, so, harder to catch.

It was an afternoon in early May when we got our first chance to test our stratagems. I was in back of the house in the shade by the well pump cleaning a couple of chickens I had killed, when I heard footsteps and then Dink's voice just above a whisper. I looked up into eyes that all of a sudden were mostly white. "What?" I said.

"It's two Yankees 'round front."

I sprang to my feet but could not say anything at first.

"Standing there by the front steps." Dink's face that was normally about the color of an eggplant was a couple of shades lighter now. "What we goan do? Better tell Mistess."

Still I hesitated. Then, my gaze leaping past him, I saw the two Yankees coming around the camellia bush at the corner of the house. Both of them had big pistols stuck under their belts. I just stood there frozen. Without saying anything they came on and stopped about ten feet away from us. They were both shabby-looking in their blue uniforms. One of them, the fat one, wasn't wearing a cap. The other one said, "Nice-looking chickens you got there."

I thought of saying thank you but didn't say anything. Dink stirred beside me, nothing more.

The fat one said, "Maybe you'd like to make a little gift to the Union army."

The other, the lean one with the jagged chin, said, "Who's in the house?"

My mother, I thought, and held it back. Some words of defiance rose but did not reach my tongue.

"Tell me, boy."

"I am." It was my mother, standing on the back gallery. She was not a tall woman, a little under the average height in fact, but standing there in her slimness three feet above ground-level with her arms lying folded and easy beneath her breasts she had a look of confident power I never had seen her wear before. Then, seeing the Yankees faced around and staring gap-mouthed up at her, I felt as if the tables were turned, the Yankees all but put to flight.

"What do you want here?" she said in a flat, not-loud voice.

One of them, the one with the jagged chin, had shut his mouth. I thought he even swallowed before he spoke. "Looking," he said. I saw that now a thought had come into his mind. It was to rest his hand on the handle of the pistol he wore, to call her attention to it. "Where's your husband?" he said.

"It is none of your business."

He hesitated but I could see his confidence coming

back. "Off with the Rebs, I bet." Then, "You a mighty uppity woman. This here place ain't yours no more. Belongs to the Union army. You Rebs is whupped."

My mother's cool blue eyes seemingly lidless and fixed on this Yankee's ugly face had not wavered a jot. But I could tell that her mind was racing. Maybe three or four seconds went by before she said, "What are you here for? To steal our chickens? I am sure your commander doesn't know what you're up to."

I saw the angry ripple of his jaw. But this time it was the fat one who spoke first. "Our commander, he don't give a hoot in hell what we do to Rebs."

"So just hold your mouth, woman," the first one said, meaner than before, resting his hand on his pistol again. "It ain't nothing to keep us from taking anything we want. Or coming in that house if we want to."

My mother's expression did not change, but she did, just for a split second, lift her gaze from his face. That was when it struck me that she had arrived at some kind of an idea. What she said was, "Don't be so sure about that."

"Yeah," the Yankee said, ugly, "I ain't seen nothing to stop us. Have you, Dan?" This with a leering grin at the fat one.

"I shore as hell ain't."

There was a pause. I knew it was coming now, whatever it was. My mother said, "Perhaps you soon will."

My mother turned (going where?) and walked deliberately to the corner of the gallery from where she could reach the rope to the farm bell on the post there. Her quick hands seized the rope and pulled, and pulled again, and again, while the Yankees stood staring as if the big bell's resonance had stunned them in their tracks. In the last shuddering echo of sound my mother's sudden voice called out, called loud for distance, "Tell them to come quick . . . all of them." Turning toward where her gaze was trained, I saw. Pompey was there, at a little distance beyond the yard fence, standing motionless this side of the garden gate.

There was a little interval before I could make sense of it. Maybe it was those blank Yankee faces that jogged my understanding and set me all of a sudden fearing that Pompey might fail to see. In fact it took him another tense second or two. Then I saw his head jerk, his body wheel and lurch into a run that quickly took him out of sight beyond the stable and the cedar thicket where the graveyard was. It was only then that I looked back at the Yankees. Both of them were looking at my mother again.

"Calling on your niggers, huh? Yeah."

My mother took his gaze as before, without expression. The fat Yankee spoke to him, words I didn't catch. But the words seemed to make a difference. The ugly one looked away, looked toward the cedars where Pompey had vanished, then back at my mother again. "All right," he said. "But them niggers won't be with you much longer."

"We'll see," my mother said. "I think you should leave right now."

He hesitated, glanced over his shoulder, looked back at her. "All right. This time." He started and, though already several steps behind the fat one, stopped again. "But your time's coming, Miz High-tone Reb. We going to get every last thing you got."

With that he turned away and, to the back of him, my mother said, loud enough to be sure he heard, "You're a little late. The Confederate army beat you to it."

Then they were gone. We, Mother and Pompey and Dink and Cice and I, standing in front of the house watched them go on down the pike on a pair of mules they had surely stolen and meant to sell. I remember thinking that if the Union army was made up of scum like those, we didn't have much to worry about in the long run.

CHAPTER TWO

Throughout 1862 and into '63 the situation locally, though hard and often frightening, was bearable. But after General Rosecrans was appointed Commander of Nashville we began to feel the whole weight and bitterness of Yankee occupation. Together with Governor Andrew Johnson, that envious and mean-spirited son of the East Tennessee mountains, Rosecrans set out to show us the consequences of our wicked rebellion against the sacred Union. The new policies of harassment he executed on us included, for example: a loyalty oath, a card index on every citizen in the county, breaking and entering houses at all hours without pretext, sending people (including women) to the penitentiary and to Northern prison camps because of their politics, confiscating livestock, rocking and shooting of houses, refusing right of burial for killed Confederate soldiers, suppression and confiscation of the press, heavy assessments on citizens, rewarding Negroes for informing, and other policies I could name. Possibly excepting New

Orleans, no other occupied Southern city had to endure so much.

Living several miles from the city was of some advantage to our family. But as the war drew on, this advantage was less and less. As the number of Yankee troops steadily increased, finally swelling the city's population to three times its pre-war level, the pressure more and more extended to include the countryside around. Yankee soldiers along the pike were now a common sight. And it came to be that some of our unwelcome visitors were there with official sanction to plunder whatever might be thought useful. Several times, without apology or explanation, such soldiers entered our house by open force, treating themselves, as it were, to a little tour of all the rooms in search of objects or persons unnamed—and of course to the terror of my two little sisters. Because of my mother's poise and astuteness they were not able to discover much that was a great loss to us, except once. It was a valuable Turkish rug that Mother had somehow failed to hide with sufficient cunning. She cried afterwards, a little, with silent tears.

Simply obtaining food enough for our own and Pompey's family was increasingly a problem. From early '64 on, our staple diet consisted of corn meal, turnips and yams, the fruit mostly of the garden we had located on the sheltered side of the hill in back of the house. Occasionally we would have some pork, from our now-wild pigs which we had to shoot like game in the woods. But most of this my mother held back for sale or for barter with neighbors, and sometimes with Yankees. In the latter case this usually meant a trip into the city. I remember those trips (they were not very many) as always frightening. And indeed, according to reliable reports, there was good reason to be afraid, especially for a woman. Still, we did it, Mother and I on that battered wagon behind those two decrepit mules.

I will never lose the vivid memory of my mother on that wagon seat with the lines in her hands, stiffly erect in a long, loose gray garment she had contrived to wear, nun-like. Her wide bonnet too was gray and so shaded her face that, as it seemed, only her bright, watchful eyes were entirely visible. The first of our trips was in early spring and most of the once-paved streets, between those somehow desolate brick and clapboard store-fronts, were a slop of mud fetlock-deep. They were crowded, though, with a tangle of wagons and caissons and mounted men nearly all in blue, and a din of rattle and splash and clamorous voices. But intermittent along the walkways of boards to either side were little pools of quiet, clusters of still white faces of men in dark clothes of everyday.

Then, turning, into a spacious lot nearly impassable with wagons and the long winding queue of people, citizens, inching and waiting and inching forward into the warehouse door. A tall, black-bearded Yankee soldier wanted to know what was under the straw in our wagon bed. My mother, about to climb down from her seat, settled coolly back. "Yams," she said.

Under the straw in fact were two pigs all cleaned and gutted, but (my mother's ruse) near the surface, overlaying the wrapped carcasses, was a solid heap of yams.

"Let's see them yams," the Yankee said and put his hand into the straw. It came out with a big half-rotten one. He looked at it. "God damn hog food," he said. "Grub for Rebs." He flipped it hard onto the ground. My mother just looked at him till he turned away.

We got good and much-needed money for those pigs and, that time, returned home without incident. We were not always so lucky. Harassment of Rebs seemed to be the favored form of Yankee humor, and though it commonly expressed itself in mere wisecracks it sometimes became more serious, designed to humiliate. Like the day two mounted Yankees, having overtaken us on our way home, rode close along beside our wagon ridiculing the bonnet my mother wore. When they got no response at all, not even the hint of an upward glance, the one riding beside her reached down and snatched it from her head. When this also failed to get a response he decided to keep it, and with mock expressions of gratitude rode off waving it merrily in the air. My mother, just as before except for the bonnet gone, with rays of the late sun illuminating the gray now mingled in her auburn hair, said not a word through the rest of that slow ride home. We never had to suffer molestation more serious than on this occasion, but there were people much less fortunate than we.

Let me say here, however, that behavior of this kind, and much worse, was by no means universal among their soldiers. Often we heard tales of kind and gentlemanly acts on the part of individual soldiers, and one, a Captain Burns from Illinois, went to considerable lengths to have a stolen milk cow returned to us. (Though in less than a month the cow was stolen again.) But such kindnesses diminished in number as the war went on and on.

In April and May of '63 there were two events very damaging, and also disillusioning, to us. As we discovered, they were connected events. The first was Cice's leaving us, without a hint of warning, simply disappearing in the night. He was not a reliable worker, but his help was much better than nothing. There were two causes, I think. One was Mr. Lincoln's Proclamation of January 1 purporting to free all slaves in the rebellious states. It was slow to percolate down, but it did so finally. The other cause was General Rosecrans' policy of rewarding slaves for informing. When a small detachment of soldiers appeared and, without so much as a nod our way, went straight back to and over the hill to where we kept our two good teams of mules, we immediately surmised what had happened. This was confirmed, very reluctantly and with shame, by Pompey. Loss of the mules was a blow, but the fact of Cice's betrayal was almost a greater one.

Of course this was beginning to happen generally, especially among the younger slaves, the males. From our present perspective, thirty-five years later, this defection of slaves should not have come as a surprise to us. But it did, a surprise informed by considerable disillusion. At least in our part of the South, and in most parts, I believe, the great majority of owners of slaves (numbering certainly fewer than one-third of all families) did not, as the Abolitionists insisted, see their slaves as 'chattel.' In fact for most owners they were, in a special sense, family. Increasingly as the years go by, this description of the relationship has come to seem, especially in the North, a largely fictitious one, an empty attempt to justify the Peculiar Institution. Nevertheless this description is very close to the facts. The intimacies common among us (I do not mean intimacies of a sexual kind) were, though qualified, indeed family-like. Hence our feeling of betrayal when defections began to occur.

Here I suddenly find myself digressing into the realm

of polemics. I feel, however, in light of the recent and growing tendency to factual distortion by historians and others, that certain things cry out to be said in our defense. The first is that few among us would restore the Institution if we could. We can see now that its defects far outweighed its virtues, not only in economic terms (which terms perhaps may not have applied in big-plantation country) but in other and more important respects as well. Surely chief among these defects was the very ground of slavery: the long-accepted right of a man to power in all things over the sovereignty of another. Which meant the right to break up families when need be, to punish at will and to other abuses much advertised, and much exaggerated, in the North. It also led to legal confusion, the contradiction involved in the effort to define and establish the legal rights of a person, a slave, who by law was not fully a person.

This much in condemnation must be said, but it is only fair also to view the matter through the eyes of the slaveholders themselves. I have already mentioned the family-like relationship between slave and master, though, for the argument's sake, I should have included the admission that obviously it did not exist in all cases. As there are bad people in all conditions of life, so were there bad masters. But I would contend that the number of these has been vastly, often deliberately, overstated. For the most part these truly bad masters were reviled and in some instances prosecuted by law. Such prosecutions are the clear evidence for the increasingly successful efforts throughout the South to support by established law humane treatment of slaves. And for further evidence of generally humane treatment one may consult the many recent interviews with former slaves, a

majority of which, even allowing for nostalgic embel-
lishment, testify to the same.

Look at it this way: the institution of slavery was an in-
herited one, passed down from time immemorial to the
first American settlers at Jamestown and hence to us.
Until the latter Eighteenth Century, critics of the institution were hard to find, even among New Englanders,
some of whom in early days adopted it for their own and
also traded in it. Moreover, according to the lights of our
Bible-centered religion, slavery clearly had divine sanction. Why the South did not continue in the apparent intention of that first generation of settlers to reject slavery
is at least understandable. I assume that economics
played the larger part, but there was much more.

The South was by no means alone in seeing the black
slave as a primitive child of Africa requiring, if he ever
was to be fully civilized, generations of schooling in the
white world. In spite of recent Yankee historians and excepting a minority of loud Abolitionists, the North held
much the same view. Evidence for this assertion may be
adduced from many sources, not least of which is the
abundance of recorded opinion expressed by soldiers of
the invading Union army. Lincoln, in his 1858 debates
with Stephen Douglas, spelled out in unambiguous detail his own like-minded view of the matter, and the
savage slaughter of scores, if not hundreds, of innocent
Negroes in the streets of New York City in 1863 can
only be seen as still more powerful evidence of Northern
attitudes.

Largely financial reasons and not slavery caused the
war. Lincoln's Proclamation, by his own admission, was
a late, desperate but successful device to revive the flag-
ging support of the Northern people . . . who were

handed therewith a banner proclaiming Holy War. Few in the Confederacy ever doubted the justice of their cause, on grounds of slavery or Constitutional right or other grounds, and the invasion of Northern armies only strengthened a will already determined to resist.

And one point more. Given an educated choice between Southern slavery and the wretched sweatshops then prevailing, many a Northern laborer might well have chosen the former.

CHAPTER THREE

*I*n the course of the war, from the time of my father's enlistment in early '62 on, we received only six letters from him. The means of delivery were always uncertain, the letters often passing through several hands and, especially in our kind of situation, fraught with danger for the bearer. I remember finding one of the them pinned to the inside of the barn door because, even in the night, the unknown bearer was afraid to approach the house. Another time one came to us by Pompey's hand. Back on the far hillside where Pompey was digging turnips a boy came out of the woods and gave it to him. "I don't recollect ever seeing him before," Pompey said. "Come from back in them hills someplace, I reckon," gesturing with his battered hat toward the hills west of us. "Wouldn't tell who sent him."

It was the letter that told us Father had been wounded (at Shiloh, we figured) and I watched the tears coursing down my mother's now-hollowing cheeks as she read. But he was healing fast, the letter said, and he would be joining the army again soon. Where? He didn't tell us.

Two times, in '62 and again early in '63, Father came home, stealing in on foot through the night. He appeared, that first time, like an apparition at the kitchen door, pinched and exhausted-looking in a shabby black coat that was too small for him. But it was he, his arms embraced me. He slept through most of the following day, on a pallet in the back room of Pompey's cabin, while Ella and her two small children hovered silently around, gawking at him, making sure his blankets stayed in place. Dink and I, and Mother too, were never far away, poised and watchful as hawks. An hour after dark he was gone again, leaving behind him a feeling of void like air grown hard to breathe.

His second time at home lasted much longer. He was sick, so sick that we marveled how he could have walked so far. (It was from Murfreesboro, where a recent battle had been.) This time, because the Yankee troops were on the alert, Mother decided that in spite of the cold he would be safer in the barn. We cleared a space in the hay in the barn loft and kept him wrapped in quilts and blankets and warmed with hot bricks we brought from the house every hour or so. Bringing in a doctor was out of the question, but Mother, a pretty good doctor, herself, knew all manner of remedies for such as fevers and aches and infections. In about three days, though still very weak, he was not flushed with fever anymore. My mother stayed every night with him, wrapped in the same covers with him, and would have stayed through the days too except for her duties in the house. And except for her fear also, for snooping soldiers might come to the house and wonder at her absence.

Not that Father lacked for company during the day. I was the one most with him, but sometimes it would be

Pompey or Ella, and of course, though much too small to tend him, both of my little sisters. His deep blue eyes, darker-seeming than they used to be, would brighten when they came, and he would hold them, sometimes both together in his arms. Over and over he would call their names. "Kate," he would say, "pretty Kate," and, "Liza, just as pretty, with all this golden hair." Both of them, especially Liza who was only three, were afraid of him at first. It was no wonder: his long tangled hair and beard and the tremor about his lips gave him a strange, wild look.

By the third day his mind was clear and in a voice that failed sometimes he talked to me at length, asking questions but not answering most of mine. It was because he did not want to talk about the war, the horrors he had seen. "I'll tell you someday, son," was as much as he would say. In silences, half-reclining on the hay close beside him, I would listen to the sough of wind on the shingled roof overhead and feel its bitter gusts across my face.

Sometimes Pompey was there with us, seated beside me, leaning forward now and then to draw the quilt still closer around my father's body. I watched his black hands working, as tender as a girl's. "Don't you have no worry," he would say, "We taking good care, watch them all the time. Eve'ything goan be fine, fine."

He grew up with my father, a couple of years older but Father's steady companion when they were young, as Dink was mine. He was not as tall as Father but greater by far in bulk, and especially after Father left for the army I always thought of those muscular arms and shoulders as protection for us all. There were times when, in reference to Pompey, the word 'slave' came

into my mind. It always came with a faint stroke of surprise, as though it were not true, not of Pompey. I knew
of cases, though not very many, in which local owners
had whipped one of their slaves. But imagining such a
thing in Pompey's case, and Father with the whip in his
hand, was more like a scene in a nightmare than an image
of the possible. It could almost as soon have happened
to my mother. Once Father did threaten to whip Cice,
Pompey's elder son, but Pompey took care of it, and
meaningfully. Whatever may have been there deep in
Pompey's heart about his condition was never allowed to
surface.

Another week and Father was all but at himself again.
He wanted to leave then but Mother persuaded him to
put it off for at least another two days. This postpone-
ment was almost a catastrophe. They came, five of them
on horseback. I saw them coming along the pike and
somehow even before they reached our gate I felt a jolt of
alarm. Then at our gate they stopped. I saw an arm
pointing our way. I was on the front porch and I wheeled
and bulled the door open and ran through the hall to the
kitchen. "They're here," I said, almost screamed it.
Mother, at the cook stove, dropped with a shocking
thump on the floor the skillet from her hand.

I remember Mother's face, suddenly white as a
leper's, saying, "Go to Father," and my lunge for the
back door where Ella with her mouth open stood half-
blocking the way. Bumping past her and out at the door
I hit the ground already running with all my strength. I
vaulted the barnyard gate, then into the hallway and up
the ladder to the loft. "They're here! The Yankees!"

Father was sitting up, a blanket over his shoulders.

Instantly I saw, gave thanks, that Pompey was with him, and now, suddenly, on his feet.

"There's the fork." It was Father's voice, his hand was pointing, he too was up. Pompey in two strides reached and seized the fork and I, seeing Father already in motion, remembered the plan we had settled on. A few quick steps to one of the feed-holes down into a stall manger and Father had his legs in and then his body, out of sight. Pompey was ready with a fork full of hay, and then another. Father's voice, muffled in the hay now covering him, said, "Put it over those blankets too. And get out of the barn quick . . . and clear of it."

Not three minutes later we, Pompey and I, were out and into the orchard between the barn and the smokehouse. That was when we saw the Yankees, three of them, standing at the foot of the steps onto our back gallery. Though looking our way they did not appear to see us. Then I could tell they were looking elsewhere, looking toward the barn, and in that same instant they started for it.

What could we do but watch, following with our eyes the three quick-stepping blue figures, two with rifles swinging in their hands, approach and enter the barn lot and then the twilight area inside the open door. There came a little interlude, a stillness broken only by the sound of chickens cackling somewhere near the barn. I heard a voice, another in answer, but nothing like calls of alarm. Soon I could tell that they were up in the loft, because I could see in the bay window dust rising from the hay. "They're poking in the hay," I murmured to Pompey.

"Sho is," Pompey said, so low I could barely hear him.

Then, like a long-held breath released, it was over. The three of them came out of the barn and followed a route that took them to the chicken house and the smoke house and even to the privy for hurried glances inside. They spotted Pompey and me but passed us by and joined up with the other two soldiers approaching from up toward Pompey's cabin. Standing near the chimney on the visible side of our house, they consulted for a minute or two. Then they were gone. In the night of the day after, in misting rain, Father set out on his long and dangerous walk back to the army.

The worst times, of course, were yet to come. The year of '64 was much harder than '63 had been, not only because of the constant strain of merely maintaining life and tolerable health among us but also because of the news. It came to us by the grapevine of neighbors up and down the pike, by report and misreport, and by the always suspect accounts to be found in the Nashville papers. It was clear, however, that things were bad and likely to get worse. The result of the battles around Chattanooga in the fall of '63 was ominous. It was retreat, always slow retreat despite the gallantry of our army. By the following summer Atlanta, that crucial city, was threatened. Then came Kennesaw Mountain in June and a month later Atlanta's fall.

Of course we had our intervals of hopefulness, inspired by reports, sometimes mistaken, of Confederate successes and deeds of heroism. And also of course there was the great General Lee in far-off Virginia whose outnumbered army seemed more than a match for the hordes of Grant and Sheridan. There were constant, groundless rumors about Lee's intentions: he would come in person and take command of the Army of Tennessee; he was planning a great sweep south to make one army of the two. Such were the wraiths we entertained, in the face of oncoming ruin.

I do not think that my mother, certainly not after Atlanta fell, ever gave any serious credit to the popular delusions. She pretended to do so and often for the sake of those around her wore a bright and convincing semblance of hopefulness. Even the reports that came in November of Lee's now-diminishing success in Virginia did not visibly ruffle her determined public demeanor. I saw behind it, though. She was a religious woman and had the habit of prayer, but now the habit had become almost an obsession. Even in company sometimes I would suddenly notice her parted lips, her face uplifted a little. Again, as I could not remember happening in the past, I would find her alone somewhere in the house, on her knees. A couple of those times she had turned her head and looked up at me with wet glistening eyes, all her bitter anxiety plain in her face.

At such times I would try to comfort her. In fact I was well suited to do so, for in my heart I never could believe that defeat was possible, much less that my gallant father could suffer any permanent harm. Someday he would come back, mounted on that same handsome claybank gelding, the light of victory floating like an aura around his head. I would say to her, "Please don't worry, Mama, please. God won't let it happen. I know it. I know it. He told me." Then she would get to her feet and embrace me, holding my head close in the hollow of her neck.

Well on in November the word came to us that the Confederate army had crossed the Tennessee River and was advancing, with little resistance, straight north toward Nashville. Whatever it really meant, this was excitement for us, though excitement still mixed with anxiety. Wouldn't there be a battle here, a Confederate attack upon all those elaborate fortifications formed in a half-circle around the city? I had seen the cannons, walled-in on hilltops, commanding the country around. The vision of those guns belching smoke and flame, and our lines at full cry under the battle flags charging head-on and heedless of all that thunder was one that in turn would chill my blood and again would set it racing. And Father would be in it, would he not? Given the brief letter we received about this time, there was every reason to think so.

But also about this time there was, especially for my mother, more than only this to think about. In the course of a week all of us, including Pompey's family, fell victim to the grippe. (Such was the name we called it by.) For some of us, for Pompey and his children and me, it was only a matter of a few days' harsh discomfort. But for Mother and Ella and especially my little sisters it was a persistent and scourging affliction. The one hit hardest of all was Liza, the younger and least robust of the girls, and even after the others, including her sister, had made partial recoveries she lay there limp and wasted, by turns flushed with fever or white as the pillow her head lay on. Merciless fits of coughing would seize her, ending in dry heaves that racked not only herself but Mother and me. Three times I was sent to town for a doctor, walking all the way, but I never was successful. Not only was sickness near-rampant in the city also; there was the ferment of military preparation inspired by the approach of the Confederate army.

So we (that is to say, Mother, who was still half-sick

herself) did the best we could with household remedies that now-a-days begin to seem quaint to us. I remember calomel and turpentine and certain herbs as playing a part in the remedies my mother used, and it may be that the potions she concocted for Liza were of some help. Though maybe not; it may have been only in the nature of her illness, whatever its proper name, that she would have lengthy spells of seeming much better, then lapse again. We had moved her little bed into the kitchen near the cookstove, the warmest place in the house, and Mother spent the nights on a pallet close by Liza's bed.

In the midst of this came unexpected news. We had supposed that the next great battle would occur only when the army reached the neighborhood of Nashville, at the least some days, or possibly weeks, in the future. But this one had already happened, at Franklin twenty miles south. We learned that Confederate losses were heavy, but the real extent of the damage done was obscured by the fact that in the battle's aftermath our army was still advancing toward Nashville. To me especially, who read the fact as clear evidence that we had scored a victory, this was hopeful, this was exciting news. Never mind the losses, Father was not among them. This unwarranted assumption, with which I sought to reassure my mother, a little later was confirmed. Again through Pompey, a message was conveyed to us. "Told me tell you Master's all right, not to worry. Say, just pray for him." In fact, considering the real condition of our army, he was in need of our prayers. I was soon to find out in person that Hood, the reckless and now-desperate general who had replaced General Johnston shortly before Atlanta fell, was commanding a decimated, ragged, hungry and demoralized army.

But desperate or not, within days after the disastrous battle at Franklin the general was busy investing the hills circling Nashville on the south, preparing what was meant to be a merely temporary siege of the city preliminary to attacking it. If Hood was a desperate man I doubt that he was more desperate than my mother was at this time. From the moment when we got word that Father had survived the fighting at Franklin, she began to hope, then to anticipate, that he would come home. And now, supposing that he was not more than a few miles away in those hills to the south, she began to truly expect him. I would observe, even through those intervals when she was gently tending her now-dangerously feeble daughter, her look of strained attention, as though she might at any moment hear her husband's footfall on the gallery. If only, her expression said, if only he would come. And I would think, "Maybe he will," and then, "But how could he stay, and what could he do for Liza?" And there were times, more and more of them, when I thought that it was not Liza but Mother whose life might depend on his coming.

CHAPTER FOUR

*I*t was maybe an hour before daylight on December 13 when I, along with Dink, set out on my mission. Winning my mother's permission had required whole days of persuasion, persuasion that most likely would have failed but for a crisis, still another crisis with Liza. In the wake of it, her child snatched back from the edge once more to fragile breath and life, my mother's wan face looked up at me. Then, the words not really audible, her lips said it. "All right. You may go." She had not finished wavering yet, however, and once or twice in the hours remaining she all but reversed her decision.

Despite my mother's state of mind she managed to give me, in clear order, such information as she had gathered and advice about the danger. She even drew a little map that I studied, then stuffed in my pocket . . . in among the cornpones and a couple of baked potatoes. I made promises. At the kitchen door I vowed to return by the night of the following day. I did not, could not meet her blear eyes as I drew my hand from hers.

Up to a point I was already familiar with the route

she had outlined for me. Some two miles farther out the pike, just beyond the ford there, was a turn-off into a lane that ran south past the Henderson farm and on toward a valley between wooded hills. That, she believed, would take us, after another mile or so, to a point at least even with and maybe a little past the west end of the Confederate line of entrenchments. From that line west to the river, she thought, there were only a few scattered Confederate redoubts, and probably only detachments of Yankees to stand as counter to these. So, in the dark and by keeping alert, when daylight came we should find ourselves in Confederate territory. Then east to where the bulk of our line began near the Hillsboro Pike.

The thing we had most seriously failed to take into account was the weather. For some days without interval it had been very bad, with mingled rain and sleet. We had dressed for this, both Dink and I, in coats rudely cut from canvas, on top of our woolen ones. But this day's approaching daybreak discovered to us an unexpected addition to rain and sleet. Because our progress on the muddy pike was slow and because of a near-invisible mounted detachment of splashing, clinking Yankees from which we had to hide, we did not reach the ford until it was time for daylight. But there was no daylight, not in the usual sense. There was a faintly luminous but still blinding fog that was, if anything, more deceptive than darkness. We could just make out the glimmer of water in the ford, and stopped.

"Don't want to get in that water," Dink said. Only the faceless shape of him was visible beside me. "I think it's a down tree across . . . yonder."

We stepped off the road, feeling our way on ground

that was half-frozen. The tree was there and we, because of our blindness, crawled across on hands and knees. Back on the pike again I said, "That lane's not but a little ways on," hearing my voice a whisper.

But the lane was hard to find. Once, deceived by the fog, I turned and stepped off the road. But it was a ditch, with bitter water ankle-deep under the sheen of ice.

"You get wet?"

"Just my foot."

We went on, slowly, our eyes scouting just ahead where only glimmering puddles defined the surface of the road. Then, like an accident, we discovered the lane, the way indistinctly framed by the massive trunks of two trees. "Come on, we need to hurry," I said, my voice a whisper still.

We walked a little faster, with more assurance now because most of the time the way was like a channel walled by nearly solid thicket; this and also because we were leaving the dangerous pike behind us. When on our right the thicket broke off I supposed we were passing the Henderson farm. I was sure when I heard a dog bark, that kept on barking until we came where again solid thicket closed in.

"Wonder where them Yankees passed us went."

"I don't know," I said.

"Reckon they come this way?"

I hadn't thought to examine the ground. "Wait." I got down on my knees. With my eyes close to the ground and with my hands I easily made them out, hoofmarks, many of them, some gouged inches deep into the wet earth. "Yeah. We ought to of known . . . from stepping in them."

After a moment of silence, a strangely perfect silence that seemed to be caused by the fog, Dink whispered, "We best get off this lane."

"And fight through all that brush . . . making noise?"

"Have to go slow. Beats walking in amidst them."

Still on my knees I thought for a minute. "Naw. We just go quiet, they can't see us. We hear them or something, we can get off in the bushes."

So we went on as before, just more cautiously still.

The lane had begun to climb and this, that we had reached higher ground, was why we received a sudden flush of gray daylight in our faces. It was only a pocket in the fog but it stopped us cold in our tracks with the feeling that now we stood exposed. Eyes in the fog-bank looking out at us? Dink's voice whispering, "We best get in that thicket."

I hesitated. "I don't hear nothing."

Dink's eyes were open wide, looking white. I said, "They'd be bound to make some noise . . . all those men and horses. If they were anywhere close. Come on."

The lane continued to climb, in solid fog again, and soon we felt the ground come level under our feet. Then, in another pocket of gray light, we had real cause to stop. It seemed to me that what I saw, all I saw, was the barrel of a musket, then two of them, suspended in the bank of fog with muzzles fixed hard upon us. But there were shapes behind them, men like shadows until they stepped forward into our circle of daylight.

"Put those hands on top of your head."

We did it, quick. The one that had spoken, the taller one, lowered his musket and stepped across the space between us. He stood a foot taller than I, looking narrowly down into my face. Then his free hand came up and, dislodging my own hands, snatched the hood of canvas off my head. He did the same with Dink and stood looking into one and then the other of our faces. "God damn kids," he said, his Yankee voice like a whip cracking. "What're you doing here?"

For a space I could think of nothing at all, and when I did it made no believable sense.

"Speak up, boy." His voice was even more like a whip. This time it stung a fool answer out of me.

"We were going . . . somewhere."

"Yeah, where?"

I didn't dare tell him the truth, and no lie came to mind. I was aware of my mouth hanging open.

After a pause the Yankee, without turning his head, said to the other one, "We better take them in, Lige. Might amount to something."

I don't know how long we walked. It seemed a timeless sort of progress, along a wide well-beaten path through thicket and then a belt of big trees whose trunks I could just make out—hickories, I thought, as though it mattered—then up a sudden incline to where I saw in the thinning fog vague shapes of soldiers moving about and a kind of long mound with a trench behind it. And a cannon, two of them.

The tall soldier walking ahead led us up to where three other soldiers stood beside one of the cannons. When they turned our way the tall soldier saluted. "Sir. We caught these back down there in the trail. A white and a black one. They ain't said why yet."

The three of them looked us over. One, with a long hooked nose, in a wide-brimmed hat and coat with brass buttons on it, finally said, in a voice with a hint of a threat, "What're you boys doing here?"

I still could think of no lie that would do. To no purpose I opened my mouth and closed it again. The point-
less fact that now sleet was falling on my still-unhooded
head somehow registered with me.

"You, black boy," the officer said. "What are you
doing here?"

Dink made a small throttled noise with his mouth. He
tried again and it came out clear enough. "I's with him."
Dink looked as if he might be expecting a bullet between
his big walled eyes.

The officer stood gazing at me, a long ruminant gaze.
"You know what we do with spies? We shoot them."

"We ain't spies." I had just managed to get it out, but
he heard it all right.

"What are you, then? Out with it."

"Captain Mercer," somebody called out. That was
my officer's name, because he turned away from me and
waved in answer. When he looked back it was the tall soldier he was addressing. "Take them up to my tent. Tell
Sergeant Gates to search them. I'll be there in a little
bit."

It was much more than a little bit, however; it was
hours, or seemed to be. At least we were out of the
weather, sheltered from the sleet that fell with a rustling
whispering sound on the canvas close over our heads.
But the board bench to which we were sentenced was
torture by and by, and even our squirmings in search of
relief were brusquely cut short by that sergeant. "Get
still!" he would suddenly, brutally say, lifting his eyes
from the barrel-head that served him for a desk.

This was all he would say, and all he had said since our
first minutes with him. That was when he had wrested
my secret from me. The little map my mother had drawn

he found in my coat pocket. Damning evidence—or so, in that moment, it seemed to me. He studied it briefly. It was when he looked up at me hard with his question that I came out with it, about my father, my little sister. His only response was to keep on looking at me for another little while, then at Dink and back to me. Then he had said, "Sit down on that board there and keep still."

So we sat, an hour, two hours, seeing through the open tent-flap soldiers walking past and other soldiers made distant by the falling sleet, with picks and shovels rising, glinting, falling as they worked. Chunk, chunk was the sound, and sometimes voices never very loud. We dared not speak even in whispers to each other, except the speech of glances meant to reassure ourselves.

In the end we never even saw the officer again. We saw the sergeant suddenly get up from his drum head and go outside and we heard his voice and that of another out there in quiet conversation. But we did hear the last of their words, that must have been those of the officer. "Take them down to the pike and head them home. And tell them to stay there, by God, before they get shot by one army or the other."

Seconds later there was a soldier looking into the tent at us. "You boys come on." I think it was his voice, before I could even see him clearly, that identified him to me. It was a black man.

I am practically sure that Dink had heard of black soldiers in the Union army, but I don't think it had ever really registered with him, not till now. There was misting rain but no obscuring fog anymore and on our way back to the pike Dink couldn't keep from glancing back time and again at the soldier: a big one as black as he was, walking a little behind us with his musket angled over his shoulder. We were both past being afraid by now, but Dink had almost the look of somebody out for his morning walk. So far he hadn't said anything, nor had the soldier. We were not too far from the pike when I heard Dink's voice.

"You a Yankee nigger?"

"I ain't a nigger, I'm a colored. Sho I'm a Yankee."

Except for the sloshing sound of our feet there was silence. Then,

"They make you come be a soldier?"

"Naw," the deep voice said. "I j'ined up by myself. Nobody make me do nothing."

Another silence, longer this time.

"You ain't never been a slave?"

The word, in Dink's mouth here and now, was a kind of shock to me. I looked obliquely at his face, hearing the black man say,

"Never was. I's born free." And then, "How come you ain't free? All you got do is walk away. Mister Lincum done freed you long time ago."

Dink didn't answer. His face had a studying look that didn't tell me anything, that kept me feeling uncertain and troubled the rest of the way to the pike. There, come to a stop, the soldier said, "Get yourselfs on back home. And don't come back this way no more. You lucky you didn't get killed."

I started away, with Dink a step behind me. Then I stopped because he had. He had turned half around to say, loud enough for the black man to hear him, "I'm a Confed'rate."

Then we went on up the pike together.

CHAPTER FIVE

Until we had rounded the first bend in the pike neither of us said a word. Then, "What we goan do now?" Dink said. "Goan back home?"

He stopped walking when I did. The falling rain was more than a drizzle now, dripping from the canvas hoods that sheltered both our faces. His gaze, diverted from me, wavered for a moment, settled someplace up the pike as if home were visible there. "Them woods and hills full of Yankees, I bet."

I thought about it, and then about Mother and Liza's drawn white face. Maybe dead, already dead, her blue eyes fixed and staring. "You want to go home?" I said, just conscious of my words that now brought Dink into focus again.

"If you does," Dink said. His black face was troubled, his lips stirring uncertainly.

After a moment I said, "You don't have to. Go with me, I mean. It's not . . ." 'Your fight,' I had almost said, and caught it back in time. 'Slave.' I recalled that uncomfortable moment on the lane with the black soldier. I said, "It's not something you have to do. I wouldn't blame you. We could get killed."

"I ain't afeard if you ain't." Then, "I'm a Con . . ."

Boom! It jolted us out of our tracks. A distance up the pike, just where it curved, were mounted soldiers in confusion. I caught just a glimpse of one flat in the mud by his prancing horse.

"Come on!" I said, lunging into the wet ditch, then up the bank into bushes there. He was beside me, crouching with me. Then another shot, two of them, from up the thicketed hillside. A voice shouted. Galloping horses were headed our way, some of them shearing off the pike into the hillside thicket. "Come on!"

It was a surprise, a corn patch, with dead stalks not thick enough to wholly shield us from view and deep mud to suck at our driving feet. But the woods were not far. We lunged on staggering, crashing the stalks in our path. Then two shots, at us it seemed, and then the last pitch of our strength delivered us into the sheltering woods.

Where we finally stopped and sat down heaving and heaving was the foot of a slope where cedars grew thick and great chunk-rocks from a bluff above lay scattered. It would do for now. In fact, for as long as we went on hearing sounds, muffled voices in the near-distance, we could not bring ourselves to move. But at last, except for rain, the silence healed around us. "We can go on now if we want to," I said, a little above a whisper.

"Which-a-way?"

I looked around me at the woods, tried to think. Then, "Let's eat something."

"Sho suit me."

In both big pockets of my coat I had hard-baked potatoes and pones of corn bread all broken now. "Here," I said. "We got to go easy on it, make it last."

"I hopes it do."

"I hope it do too." This voice, out of nowhere, made me let go the potato I had at my mouth. The voice added, "I could use some of that myself if you don't mind."

My first thought was that the man standing maybe ten steps away could only have dropped, rifle and all, out of that cedar tree above his head. From the looks of him, in fact, he might have been living in it for months and months getting skinnier and more ragged all the time. His coat and brimmed hat looked like ones you would put on a scarecrow after the first scarecrow had worn them out. Even his shoes, if they ever had been real shoes, were tied on his feet with string and strips of rawhide.

But by now I knew who, what he was. He was the one that had been shooting at the Yankees, a Confederate sniper soft-stepping as a wild Indian. Without a word I picked up my potato and held it out to him. He came and took it and squatting down bit off almost half of it. I watched his gaunt jaw working. His eyes under lids half-closed looked green and fever hot. He swallowed. "What the hell you kids doing out here?" His gaze touched Dink, then back to me. "Lucky you ain't both laying dead in the mud."

"I got to find my father. In Cheatham's Corps. Tenth Tennessee, we think."

"Well this ain't no time to do it. It's going to be a helluva fight around here . . . and that in the next day or two, I figure. You and your boy, here, better get back home quick and stay there." He bit into the potato again.

"I got to find him. I can't go back. I got to find Cheat-ham's Corps."

Chewing, the soldier shook his head, then swallowed. "Fraid I can't help you. 'Cept just it's down the line east somewhere." He got to his feet. "First one on this end is Stewart's. You keep going past this here hill straight up that hollow southeast, you'll come on it in a couple of miles. If you don't come on some of Chalmers' ca'vary first. And some of them pickets. They what you got to watch out for, they mighty nervous. I wouldn't risk it."

In a voice smaller than I meant it to be I said, "I got to."

"Well." He hoisted the rifle over his shoulder—a fancy one, one of those Yankee repeating rifles, I reck-oned. Then he paused. "Tell you what. I'm heading up that way, the biggest part of it. I 'spect I can get you through. Come on."

It seemed more than any couple of miles. The pace his long legs set was a strain on us and there were times when to catch up we had to go at a dogtrot, heaving and stum-bling off and on. Twice we had to climb hills and, once, slog through what seemed an endless stretch of corn-field. From a hilltop we did see on the distant road ahead a detachment of cavalry just at the point of vanishing be-hind a hill, but otherwise, except for a few stray cows and some deserted-looking farmhouses, the country-side appeared empty.

Ahead of us the soldier finally stopped. It was at the far edge of a patch of woods, this side of a field in which another deserted-looking farmhouse stood. He took a rag out of his coat pocket and stepping into the open waved it over his head. "Come on," he called back to us. We came out and stopped behind him. He turned and waved the rag over our heads and then, with a quick "Be careful," was gone before I could think to thank him.

Two pickets almost as ragged as our guide came out of the farmhouse and told us what we now expected them to say.

"We can't go back," I answered, "it's Yankees back there. I got to find my father. I got to. In Cheatham's Corps."

They looked at each other. "My God," one of them, the bearded one, said. Then, "Well, nothing for it but let them go."

He got a piece of cloth from in the house and with a stick made a little flag for us to carry, then pointed us to a wooded ridge where a pall of smoke hung against the sky. "Just keep right out in the open all the way across. And a word or two to Jesus might not hurt."

That sounded like good advice and just before we entered the woods at the foot of the slope I told Dink to say some prayers too. But it didn't seem that we needed them. I had expected undergrowth of the kind that by partly hiding us as we climbed might make them take us for spies or something. Starting a little way up the slope, however, almost everything except the larger trees had been cut away. Even some of the big trees were down, but mainly this was for the purpose of making bunkers, with deep ditches behind the fallen trunks. Half-way up we passed a crew with picks and shovels digging another one. They looked up, watched us go by. We reached the crest in the last minutes of good though cloudy daylight.

I have described the look of the sniper who guided us, and mentioned the raggedness of the two pickets at the farmhouse. But somehow the look of them had not prepared me for my first sight of our army. For a long time I had been hearing that our soldiers were badly in need of all kinds of supplies, which I thought of as meaning, mainly, good enough food and such as decent uniforms and boots. Even so, when I envisioned them, in battle or in camp, the pictures in my mind's eye were always of men in gray, lean and a little tattered and battle-worn perhaps, but men nevertheless suffused with a certain aura of stern and invincible resolution. This was not what I saw here in the flesh.

Left and right along the almost level ridgetop were campfires with men under a pall of smoke huddled around them. I could see tents, but not very many, and what at first appeared to be brush piles, dozens of them, but in fact were crude lean-to's. Along the lip of ground where the slope dropped off, cannons stationed at intervals of a stone's throw pointed down at the open field and the farmhouse in the distance. There were a few unsaddled horses standing under a tree by a tent and, much closer, half a dozen motionless mules standing in harness around a big wagon with a canvas top. They were pitiful-looking mules, all hip bones and ribs and raw harness scars: it hurt me to look at them. But the hurt was not as intense, nor even of the same kind as what I felt when, from up close, I looked at the bearded men huddled around the fires.

I remember my surprise when our approach, even when we drew very near, seemingly prompted nothing more than indifferent eyes lifted to take us in. Or not quite that, even . . . not 'in.' It was more as if Dink and I were merely the objects on which their idle gazes stopped, held for a moment, then moved on to another. Eyes that seemed without any special color, except maybe the color of the twilight coming down. Ghostly was the word that came into my mind.

That was how it seemed, though moments later when one from the huddle closest by said, "Boy, you want to come in by the fire?" I felt a little comforted. That was the moment when I also felt, as sudden as a gust of bitter wind, how cold I was, and tired as I had never been before. Drawing Dink along I entered the little circle and squatted down. "Here," the man next to me said, slipping a little sideways, "it's room up on this log." I took the place beside him.

Then, from a face beyond the fire, came the expected question. I spoke my little piece, that fell into an interlude of silence. Then, "Cheatham's is down there on the far end, ain't it?" It was the man beside me.

"Yeah," another one said. "Out there other side of Stephen Lee's. Can't tell him nothing about the Tenth, though . . . might not even be anymore. All them pieces of regiments they run in together after Franklin. Anyhow, boy, it's too big a risk for you to go wandering around out there."

"Sho is," the first man said. "Them pickets all nervous as cats."

All their eyes were on me, studying. I didn't try to answer, and in the long stillness afterwards the matter seemed forgotten. It was then, because Dink on the ground at my side had extended his shod feet toward the fire, that I first grew conscious of other feet in the circle—bare feet! And not just a pair but three of them: swollen, scarred and discolored, useless-looking feet. I looked away, then back at their clothes. Men in rags, in bitter ice and rain, soldiers. How could they fight! But nothing like the distress I felt showed in the listless faces.

Night was coming on. A hand with a stick of wood reached and poked the fire, raising a little tumult of sparks that survived for a second or two. Beyond us, by other fires, were other faces like these. The remote hum of their voices, of which I was conscious now, a little soothed my distress somehow.

"Lee," one of the men with bare feet said. "I thought he was one of them got it at Franklin. Him and about half his corps."

"Naw," another one said. "He's out there with us. Good thing, too, with all the generals and such killed and took prisoner down there. That little Lieutenant Graves said it was twelve of them, generals. And a whole bunch of others up in the ranks. They's some commanding brigades and regiments now that ain't never commanded nothing bigger'n a burial detail before."

The man with the stick poked at the fire again. He was the one that said, "It wasn't no need of that. Charging right straight at them like that. Crazy. God knows how many of us went down." He paused, tossed his stick onto the fire. "And the best friend I ever had was one of them. Wasn't ten feet away from me. A ball took his whole head off."

They fell silent . . . all, I guessed, with visions in their minds' eyes.

"They say old Forrest tried to stop him, cussed him. Fool Hood wouldn't listen." The beard of the man who spoke looked as if it had been cut off with a bayonet. He was one of only two who seemed to own a hat.

"And now he's done sent Forrest off to Murfreesboro, tearing up railroads. Like anybody couldn't tear up a railroad. And us left lacking cava'ry enough to scare a bunch of widow women off.''

Forrest gone! I couldn't believe it.

"Maybe not. They tell me Chalmers is a good cav'ry-man. I think Forrest left some of his men with him, too. So don't go getting too damn glum." Stretching his long legs put his bare feet almost close enough for the fire to burn them. "Glum ain't good for us. Do better to count what blessings we got. Which don't look like many but you never know. Like these days of freezing rain and fog and such, look how it give us a chance to get some rest we shorely needed."

"Yeah. But it ain't going to last much longer. They're forming up down there."

"Nothing going to happen till the weather clears. So just be still and rest yourself."

For a while nobody stirred or said anything, but it seemed to me that the man's words had meant something to them all. The next thing said reflected that. It was the man with the chopped-off beard, in a tone much lighter than had prevailed till now. "I reckon it's about time they ring us up for our night feast. I can't hardly stop my mouth from watering."

"Yeah, me too. Ain't nothing like a good tin cup full of goobers. I had a potato today too. Sides of my belly ain't got back together again yet."

"Well, mine has. They's met so many times they don't even greet one another no more."

Hungry. I still had two potatoes and broken corn-pones in my pockets. I hesitated. I heard a noise, a clang-ing sound repeated several times, and all the men were suddenly on their feet moving away at quick-step. Except for one, the man who had made room on the log for me. "I reckon they can spare you and your boy a little something too."

"Thank you," I said, keeping to my seat. "We got some food. In my pockets."

"That's good." He hurried on after the others.

All I had left I halved with Dink, right down to the crumbs in my pockets, and we sat there, each on a log, stuffing it into our mouths. "I wisht we had some coffee," Dink said. "Or something wet."

"Maybe I can get us some."

But a man had come up behind Dink and stood there looking at me. He was an officer; I could tell because of his brimmed hat and his gray coat that was a little tattered but fitted to him. "You boys come with me."

He led us to his tent, where just outside the open flap a fire was burning. He told us to sit down and wait till he came back, which he finally did, with two tin cups of strong, nasty-tasting coffee . . . if it was coffee. They had told him about us. He stood there in the firelight, a silver-bearded gentlemanly-looking man, as if not quite certain what to say. Finally, "And your home's between here and the city?"

"Yes sir. A couple miles west."

"Well, you can't go home now." Then, "Here's what I want you to do. As soon as it's daylight, you head south back up this ridge to where you can see to your left down into that valley. There's a house down there about a mile from where you'll be standing. We're using it for supply. You tell them Major Flannery sent you. They'll take care of you and give you something to eat. And do just what they say . . . And don't, I mean don't, come back up this way. You've got a whole lot better chance of getting killed than you have of finding your father." Then, "You understand me?"

"Yes sir."

He stood there looking at me. Finally he said, in a changed voice, "I had a boy just about three years older than you. He was killed at Kennesaw Mountain." He turned his face away from me. Then he turned around and left.

We slept on the ground inside his tent, wrapped in one blanket close together against the bitter cold.

CHAPTER SIX

Major Flannery waked us at first hint of misty daylight and ordered us on our way in a voice that meant business. He gave us each a cup of that coffee, but nothing else. I guess he thought the promise of something to eat down there would help to assure our obedience. Anyway we did as we were told.

Because of the misting rain we could not see from the ridgetop the house in the valley down there and when we reached the foot of the hill and treeless pasture it was still invisible. But after a few steps more we heard the rattling noise of a wagon and then a voice uplifted. The voice was cursing mules, we rightly supposed, and soon we were able to discern them, two teams drawing a wagon made hump-backed by a canvas-covered load. Three figures at a slogging gait followed along behind, passing entirely out of sight in another minute or so. They were on a road, of sorts, a slough almost, and we had only to follow beside it for what seemed a mile or so before the house came into view.

Between the house and a barn there were half-a-dozen wagons, some with mules hitched to them, and men passing in and out of the house and the barn too, returning with heavy wooden boxes and barrels and stuffed towsacks. Close by were two, wheeled cannons . . . waiting, I supposed, for other teams to draw them. There was also a restless-looking officer who stood slapping his boot with a riding crop. He was the one we approached.

It was maybe a whole minute before the officer even seemed to notice us standing there at a respectful distance. When at last he acknowledged our presence it was only by the severe questioning look he fastened on us. I managed to say, "Major Flannery, back up there, he told us to come to you."

"Why, for God's sake?"

"He said you'd give us something to eat."

The officer's black-bearded face now had a look of extreme exasperation. "He think we got a charitable institution down here?" Then he said, "All right, damn it," pointing with his thumb. "Go in the house there and get you some turnips or something. Then go home."

"We can't," I said in a small voice. "There's Yankees that way."

He exhaled a quick, angry breath. "Then go stay in that barn. There's still some hay in the loft. And don't bother anybody." He abruptly turned and walked toward one of the wagons.

Except for an uncertain walk-space inside the front door the house was all but stuffed with towsacks and barrels and spills of goobers, turnips and corn meal. Up-ended pieces of furniture lay here and there among them, left by the farmer who must have found himself all of a sudden evicted. Dodging among the soldiers passing in and out we filled our pockets with all they would hold and made straight for the barn loft.

It was suddenly raining again, rain mixed with sleet and blown against the roof overhead by gusts of wind stronger and colder than before. Half buried in hay we sat eating the tough raw turnips and goobers, forcing it down our gullets. I thought of the men out there, many without shoes or hats or even decent coats, shuddering as they worked. How could they do it? No matter, though, they did it: strong men that nothing could stop. Half sick, with bellies already crowded, we burrowed deeper into the hay, hearing the voices down below and the wagons moving out.

Sitting close together for warmth, dozing off and on, neither of us said anything for a long time. Except for the wind and rainy sleet, an interval of quiet came at last. Dink stirred beside me, rustling the hay. "You 'wake?"

"Yeah."

"What we goan do?"

"Try again. We got to."

"Don't look like no use. Too many of them. Don't you reckon we could get back home someway?"

"We got to do it. Anyhow we couldn't get through now if we tried to." I thought about it. I thought of my mother and Liza, how they might be, and then of my father again. Through the loft door, barely visible in the distance, I could see the horizon of hills at the head of the valley. He was up there someplace, waiting. Waiting for me, was my next thought, just as though it were true. I recalled how, from that ridgetop, I had been able to see campfires spotted eastward along another ridge and down a long descent toward another valley. Somewhere there, toward the army's east extremity, was Cheatham's Corps. And still no battle, no sound of guns. 'Nothing going to happen till the weather clears.' These words had stuck in my mind. I said,

"They're still not fighting. Can't, till the weather clears. We got to try again. Way down the line, this time. Where that soldier said Cheatham's Corps is."

Dink's head was bent down, his expression glum, and he failed to look up at me. "How he goan get home if we do find him? All them Yankees in the way."

"He'll think of a way," I said. "I know, he always can."

I wanted Dink to answer but he did not. Waiting, I noticed that the rain and wind had slackened a little, and I thought that maybe before very long we could be on our way. But there came an interruption.

The faint noise, a muffled cough, might have got past me if it had not been repeated. I looked at Dink. He had heard it too. Leaning toward me he whispered, "It's somebody up here ain't us."

I hesitated. Behind us the piled hay crested at a point higher than my head, even when, cautiously getting onto my feet, I reached my full height. Whispering too, I said, "I can't see anybody." Though we waited for some little time the sound was not repeated. Doubtful now but still with caution I climbed up to where I could look down over the crest. It was darker down there and it took me a few seconds to make out a man's pale face returning my startled gaze. His head and all the rest of him but his face were covered with hay and sacking. He reminded me of something frightened peering out of a hollow tree. I just stood there with my gaze locked on him. Suddenly,

"Don't tell them," the man said in a hushed pleading

voice. "Please don't, they got them cannons. Like light-ning straight in your face, you can't even hear. I'll give you something. I got . . . I got a horse I'll give you. Back home. I swear. If you don't tell them."

I could think only to say, finally, "I won't." He meant, I thought, the soldiers outside, but he stopped me be-fore I could ask.

"You don't know. I been a good soldier. All the way from Shiloh. All of them. All them fights around Chat-tanooga . . . till Franklin. You don't know . . . Look." From out of the sacking around him a hand appeared, a hand missing fingers, two of them. The hand was visibly trembling. "I don't know where I lost them. Sometimes I look and it's a leg gone. Eve'ything going, a piece at a time."

"I won't tell them," I faintly said. But I was thinking that a man without two fingers could go on fighting. A leg gone? How could he be here, then?

"It were such a flash . . . all white like God Hisself done it. I thought . . . I thought it wasn't none of me left but my head. I could see. I could see old Billy Ruston laying there tore clean half in two. That's when I thought I better get out and away with what I had left. That's when I run, the night after that. So I come here, but then they come along behind me. Looking for another fight. Crazy."

Dink, who had come up beside me, whispered close to my ear, "He the one's a loony."

"You've been here two whole weeks?" I asked. "How come you didn't starve?"

"I like to have, till they come. I sneak out sometimes in the night and get me something."

Now I was sure he was not missing a leg. And a second

or two later I was more than sure, because I saw him move them, two of them, drawing them up so the shape of his knees showed through the sacking. All of a sudden the fact that he was maybe a little crazy began to seem a doubtful excuse to me. I thought of those men out there, and the food he was willing to steal from them . . . from them and the whole army that had been through the same as he had. And I thought of my father who would rather die than be a coward. I changed my mind, then changed it back. "All right," I said. "I guess I won't tell them. But they're going to catch you, up here. Soon as they feed out a little more of this hay."

The man just kept looking at me with that same plead-ing look, as though I could do something to help him if I would.

I slipped back down the hay, with Dink following, and stood looking out toward the horizon. The rain had slackened to almost nothing. I said, "It's about quit, we can go now."

"Back up there?"

"Not the same place. On down the line, like I told you. They ain't going to shoot us coming from this way . . . in the daylight."

Dink rolled his eyes away from me. "Feel how cold it getting. Getting worse'n it was."

"We can come back here for the night if we have to. Come on."

Over the years I have a thousand times in memory profoundly regretted this, my forcing him to go along. Determined though he surely was to go if I did, he was acting against his will in my behalf. No matter the bond of real affection between us, this was what it meant to be a slave. This fact, of which I was only half unconscious, was the source of my discomfort with the word 'slave,' and thus was a fact that, more closely examined, might well have led me to a different course of action. I think I could have made him stay in the barn. A couple of days and all harm most likely would have passed him by, leaving him free to go back home or anywhere else he wanted. But I needed him. He was not especially bright or physically resourceful, but he was there, as he had been all my life, a sure and certain strength where it was wanted. So it was that against his will I led him into dangers in no way his to face.

To keep that officer from seeing us leave we went out through the rear door and headed east, into a bare apple orchard and then a thicket of briars and buckbushes. At the foot of a low hill we turned back north and soon were out in that open pasture land, now at a distance east of the road where wagons in a train and also a couple of cannons in tow were visible.

The rain and sleet had stopped and we could see the pall of smoke from camp fires extending all along the ridgetop and down into the valley and up another hill and out of sight. Nearly a mile of it, I guessed, and more, much more, beyond what I could see. So many soldiers, a miles-long line like a human wall, with rifles and muskets to hand and cannons pointed against the Yankee hordes. And what were bare feet and rags and hunger to an army of men like ours, fighting men who feared no odds and never would surrender? Surging pride lifted my pulse but it brought me another thought. Would he, my gallant father, consent for any reason at all to take leave at such a time?

"What you thinking?"

I realized I had stopped. Dink was looking hopefully

at me. "Nothing," I said and set off again. Father would be the one to decide.

The high ridge was straight ahead, but angling to our right between this and another hillside, the valley, now with a scattering of big trees, continued on. The smoke was thicker there, obscuring the treetops, like a porous roof of cloud suspended over the many campfires. Then I could see a house and a few tents and tethered horses close by. As we drew near, a few soldiers warming themselves at a fire turned their bearded faces to look at us. A few steps more and I heard one of them say, "Reinforcements coming, huh."

For a minute after we came to a stop they went on looking us over. Finally, "Fore you know it we'll be down to the likes of these here," one said. "Tommy, there, is just a step on the way down." A slight movement of the soldier's head directed my eyes to a young man standing on the other side of the fire. But a mere second's scrutiny showed me that he was not a 'young man' but a boy of maybe fifteen with innocent if slightly glazed blue eyes and no more than a downy suggestion of hair on his cheeks and upper lip.

Another one said, "Tommy's all right, though. As soon to have him by my side as any man here."

Tommy's eyes gave the man a little flash of gratitude.

"You come to sign up . . . you and your boy?" the first soldier said to me.

I shook my head No. "I got to find my father."

"Yeah." Studying me the soldier pursed, then pressed his lips together. "Well, you might ought to do it in a hurry. You know whose command?"

"General Cheatham's," I said. "His name's Jason Moore. He's a captain."

"Lot of captains under Cheatham, a heap of 'em. You don't know his regiment?"

"It's a Tennessee one. It might be still the Tenth."

"Umn." The soldier pursed his lips again. He glanced around him at the musing faces. "Ain't nothing I can tell you but keep on up the line east there." He gestured with his thumb. "Cheatham's out there on the far end, last I know. Ask some officers." I started to thank him and turn away but he stopped me for a moment. "Be sure and not go too far forwards, though. Pickets out there'd likely shoot you. And get out of here back to where you come from 'fore dark. And don't you forget that."

I thanked him and we started on, followed, I noticed when I glanced back over my shoulder, by a common gaze I can only describe as wistful.

I recall that long afternoon as one of unceasing and, finally, all but desperate frustration. I had supposed that by 'line' was meant something that at least resembled the accustomed meaning of the word: a successive and more or less unbroken order of things extending on to a definite final point. In fact as it seemed to me there was no definable order. There were isolated large or small groups of soldiers, not only behind and ahead of us but also to either side, and sometimes apart at such distances as might let a thousand Yankees pass through unresisted. I saw, for example, a camp with many soldiers on a hillslope and bunkers dug and ready, while beyond them up the valley a quarter-mile at least there was barely a soul to see. So it was that our progress if traced would have made only a crazy zig-zag.

We were not much more than an hour in reaching the territory occupied by Cheatham's Corps, but it was almost the same story there. The only difference was in the lesser degree of uncertainty with which my question was answered, or else in answers confidently given that turned out to be wrong. Even when, at last, we found some Tennessee regiments, which I quickly learned to identify by their colors, our luck was not any better. We walked among them, from fire to fire where the ragged soldiers huddled, asking, scanning faces. But here we ran into trouble.

I had already stopped several officers, in vain. None of them had known, but to a man they had the same thing to say. It was that we had better get the hell out of here, and quick. Pretending to, we headed out, then circled back and to our business again. But this officer, in a fitted coat and brass on his collar, did not even pause to hear my question. He simply turned his head toward a soldier and said, "Corporal."

The burly corporal stepped closer, saluting.

Lifting his arm to point, the officer said, "Take these kids up that hollow yonder and over the ridge and see them clear on away from here." He fastened his eyes on me again. They had a mean glitter in them. "You come back in here again, I'll see you lose every inch of your hide . . . both of you. Now, get!" He turned his back and walked away.

This cost us maybe an hour out of the time we had left before night. The corporal marched us up that long hollow, past where a yoke of oxen, lashed and cursed by three soldiers, labored to draw a snub-nosed cannon up the slope. The ground was mostly frozen now, a help to our feet on the steeper climb that brought us out on the ridgetop. "Now," the heaving corporal said, once we had reached the far slope. "I'm going to stand right here and watch you down this hill and on across that meadow down there. And don't come back. Get going."

We went, but already I had a plan. Starting only a little way down was thicket plenty dense enough to hide us, and here, safely shielded from the corporal's view, I said, turning left, "Come on. This way."

Dink had stopped. He was looking obliquely at me, a way he had when reluctant to follow my wishes. "You 'member what that man tole us."

"Come on."

"It ain't no use. It too many of them. He couldn't get home now, noway. And us all wore plumb out, and cold . . . Let's go back to that barn."

"We don't even know where it's at, from here," I said. "You can go on if you want to. I ain't going to stop you." I turned and started, knowing he would follow.

Of course Dink was right, clearly right. But something, a sort of hot and reckless zeal, had got into me, growing stronger with every new frustration. Those back there behind us were Tennessee regiments, and soon, except for that officer, I would have found my father's. And easy, after that, for they would know him, could not fail to know him. So I went on, with Dink behind me, through thicket along the hillslope and around until again the big valley below became visible through the trees.

But it was only as we approached the foot of the slope that I became aware, very suddenly, of a change in things. First, I think, was a difference in the light, as though we had stepped out of gloom through an open door. It came from a rent in solid cloud over hills to the west, a blaze of burning orange that the setting sun had left. And in this blaze of light there was movement down there, of men in rough columns with muskets at shoulder arms and glinting bayonets and mounted men in single-file all headed west down the valley. Then some eloquence in the scene told me what it meant. Lifting my eyes I studied the wooded hillslope half a mile away, imagining the unseen host of blue soldiers forming up in ranks beneath the trees, emplacing cannons, drawing cavalry into line. Not yet, though, not till morning, I thought. But something else took hold of me.

Was it only the horse, the rangy claybank passing by not far out from the foot of the hill? The slim rider seemed tall enough and his posture familiar to me. I dodged past a tree that intervened. "It's him," I said, or cried, already in head-long motion down the slope. But stiff buckbushes caught my feet and threw me full-length to the ground. Untangled and up again, I could not see him now among the riders. I ran, calling, and stumbling out onto level ground, I managed barely to dodge a rearing horse. "Goddamnit, kid, get out of here!" But the furious voice failed to stop me from bolting on ahead.

For all my certainty, though, I was mistaken. I caught up with the claybank horse and rider, but only to find a grim and wind-scoured face turned to look down at me. "What the hell you doing here?" Then somebody, a soldier on foot, had me by the arm. "Come on, boy."

He pulled me out of harm's way to the thicket-edge, a big stooped man with a face that looked too old to be a soldier's. But it was a kindly face and it said to me, "Need to get you out of here, boy . . . you and him." He had noticed Dink who was standing beside me now, panting and white-eyed. "But I don't know how, be dark directly." He thought for a minute, showing when he parted his lips gapped and brown-stained teeth. "Come on."

Without thinking, just conscious of being all at once too tired to do otherwise, I followed him, with Dink behind me. He took us along the foot of the hill, in the direction opposite to the passing file of cavalry, to where finally a path led up through a thicket of scrub trees and underbrush. Farther up the slope where smoke was rising was a cluster of towering trees and just beyond them, unseen before, a short stretch of sheer rock bluff several times the height of a man. What I saw next I thought to be a cave at its base, but it was not quite that. It was merely a scooped-out place reaching maybe ten or twelve feet back under the bluff, with soldiers huddled around a fire. One of the bearded faces turned on us said, "For God's sake, Hoop" and another one said, "They something of yours?"

Our man Hoop said, "I found them down there. I can't say how come. Make place for them."

There were men enough to crowd the space, but they made room anyway, shifting to leave us the choice spot between the fire and the wall. Seated now with Dink at my side, their common gaze upon us, I mumbled some words to thank them. No answer, no sound but the crackle and spit of fire. Till finally, in a voice that seemed almost reverently soft, one said, "You live around here someplace?"

I shook my head, hearing my own distant voice answer, "Back toward Nashville." Then, feeling I owed it to them, "I'm looking for my father."

The same slow voice, though kindlier still, said, "You picked a bad time to come looking, boy."

I heard his words clearly but without consequence, like words received through the pall of sleep. After that, and after a long or short interlude in which I was conscious of nothing at all but the warmth and shuddering light of the fire near my feet, I heard other voices. But finally one prevailed, a not-loud voice, high-pitched and remote somehow and sweet almost like a girl's, singing:

> *The years creep slowly by, Lorena,*
> *The snow is on the grass again.*
> *The sun's low down the sky, Lorena,*
> *The frost gleams where the flowers have been.*

It was a song I knew but never before had truly heard . . . not like this, in such a place and time, as though it were the last and final song sung at the world's end. Then silence. But later a soldier with straw-colored hair stirred and moved his bare feet closer to the fire and said that his wife was named Lory. And so was his little girl that was two years old. "Picture-pretty," he said. "Soft brown hair. Little old angel face. God, I wisht I could see her."

"You got any boys?" another one said. He was the one with the good coat, that must have come off a dead Yankee and then been soaked in lye or something to take the color out.

"Got one. Five years old. Lory says he looks just like me. Too bad, ain't it?"

Then Hoop, across the fire from me, hugging his ragged knees, said, "I got one eighteen. He's here. Out there someplace with Chalmers' cava'ry. He's a horse-riding fool. Always was."

The silence that followed went on and on, as though this boy, the horse-riding fool, were food for deep and lasting meditation. I think I fell asleep in this silence, only to be awakened, by slow degrees, to a sound I at first mistook for a lingering dream. But around the fire heads were lifted. The sound though faint was music, from somewhere out in the night. It was that of a distant band, a Yankee band, and sometimes in a sort of elfin unison the sound of Yankee voices singing. That close, I thought, listening and listening.

"Even brought a band along with them," the man beside me said.

"Pretty good one, too," another said.

"Some of them Dutchmen, I bet. Some of them can't even talk American."

After that nobody spoke and silence closed in again.

They waked us gently out of sleep to eat the hoe cake and drink the steaming brew that only looked like coffee. Even in the depths of sleep that night, I sometimes heard, or thought I did, the popping sound of muskets fired in the distance.

CHAPTER SEVEN

The two days of my search that I have so far described remain even now extraordinarily clear in my memory. I cannot say the same for at least some considerable part of the subsequent days, even though certain of the events and interludes in that time persist in coming back with a clarity that is virtually startling. I suppose that, given the shock and terror my experience included, this is not surprising. Over the course of now nearly four years of the war I had often heard described and had further imagined many of the horrors that occur in battle. But my inner vision of these things was little preparation for experience of the things themselves. And especially in cases where such things happened to people near and dear. Events of a certain magnitude can brand themselves irrevocably into a person's memory.

As it happened, Dink and I were exactly, and up to a point comfortably positioned to observe the initial action in that two-day battle. The action was in fact a feint on the part of the Yankee army, designed to draw defensive action away from the true objective, which was the opposite, or western, flank of the Confederate line. What Dink and I observed from our position on the hillside was not the main action, but it was in all seriousness battle nevertheless.

My first awakening that morning, caused by a hand on my shoulder, was in darkness so complete that I could barely make out even the silhouette of the figure leaning over me. There were words spoken before I could understand them, but soon they were clear enough. It was Mr. Hoop, quietly saying, ". . . east, off to your right when you're facing down the slope. About half a mile, you come on a railroad cut. Get on a ways past that and you'll likely be out where you're pretty safe, if you're careful. Keep on and you'll prob'ly find a farmhouse, maybe with people still in it . . . You hearing me?"

"Yes, sir." Except for Dink's heavy breathing beside me, there was no other sound. This meant, I rightly took it, that the other men were gone.

"If it's fighting here, though, you just sit tight in this hole till it's all over. But soon as it's clear you climb up this hill and get on the other side 'fore you turn east. And keep yourse'f hid best you can. I'm leaving you a couple of hoe cakes here." He moved. Then, before my numb lips could manage even a 'thank you,' he was gone.

Against the bitter cold I drew myself still tighter around Dink's sleeping body. It was then that I noticed, though groggily, the raw stink of hide against my face. They had put it under us while we slept, wrapped us in it. I groped with my hand and pulled the loose edge of the stinking thing over both our bodies, then sank into sleep again.

"You hearing that?"

I opened my eyes in dense gray light and at once was

hearing it. Above it all was the clear sound of a bugle, but under that, prevailing when the bugle hushed, was a humming as of a multitude of voices and a rattling noise I identified as many wagons drawn in haste over the frozen ground. Then again a bugle, more than one, but now so distant as to seem like elfin bugles blowing. Standing upright in the fog I could as yet see nothing down below us.

"They fixing up to fight, ain't they?"

"Yeah," I said, whispered.

A clear voice, then another, rose sharp above the hum and clatter, and then the protracted neigh of a horse. But in that moment, as I stood blindly staring, I noticed a difference in the fog, a blush of color spreading in it. Then I jumped. The distant sound was repeated, POM, and then repeated over and over with barely an interlude. When I jumped again it was because that sound had suddenly become an affliction to my eardrums. It was our cannons, emplaced somewhere nearby, answering the Yankees. POM, POM. I covered my ears. It was then as if each shock was delivered straight up through the soles of my shoes.

"They right on top of us." But Dink had had to repeat these words before I understood him.

"Not that close. I think, up there on the hilltop." Both of us covered our ears again.

Then, as if the cannon blasts had done it, there were drifting rents in the fog and, at intervals, glimpses of men down there in column and glinting tips of bayonets . . . until the fog closed again. But now it was lifting, lifting fast, admitting great patches and streaks of sunlight in which the waiting columns stood.

There was a brief interval when I could not identify

the ripping or crackling noise that broke out in the distance. Then, concurrent with that moment when the fog seemed at one stroke swept away, I perfectly knew what it was: the continuous sound of small arms from across the sweep of the valley. It was all clear now, the long blue line advancing, halting, wavering here and there, and smoke like another tattered fog discolored with flickering tongues.

"They coming on," Dink said. "Look how many."

"We'll stop them."

But our line, dun-colored figures slowly giving ground, looked meager as against that line of almost solid blue. Then in the distance, POM, repeated again and again, and ours on the ridge above us assailing our ears in answer. Smoke-trails in the air, and great orange blooms girdled with smoke sprang up in random pattern across the field. In both lines there were intervals now, and soldiers down or staggering on to fall a moment later. Our retreat had quickened, back toward islands and fringes of thicket, men at a loping run who paused to turn and fire and on at a lope again. One who had turned at a thicket's edge went down as if a massive stone had struck him.

"They killing us!"

"Just wait. You'll see." But I said it out of a throat drawn painfully tight.

But then, remembering, I did see. Those waiting columns of ours no longer waiting, already in forward motion, were flaring out as they advanced into a battle line. And behind them now, forming into order down there, were gun crews with their cannons and the caissons and rumbling ordnance wagons as far along the line as I could see. This was the army, and those out there, as I understood now from my own small battle lore, were merely the skirmish line.

"See down there," I said to Dink. "It's coming now. That wasn't nothing but skirmishers out there." I felt the hot blood pumping through my veins.

A tight little group of mounted officers, just when my eye fell on them, split and cantering away in several directions left a single one sitting motionless there on a rangy, blood-bay horse. I dismissed the thought that it was my father, but he would look like that: tall and straight in his saddle, in brimmed hat and long gray coat and a hand at rest on the saber at his side. Surveying the field, the advancing line, his head turned slowly east and west, then ceased to move at all. General Hood himself? I thought, dismissing this thought too because I knew of Hood's missing leg. In that same moment the officer's horse began to prance and the silver glint I abruptly saw was the saber drawn from its scabbard.

That was the moment. A keen bugle sounded, then others down the way, and the line of dun-colored soldiers and glinting bayonets was suddenly in motion, then faster, a vaguely crouching, loping gait that seemed at one with the shrill cry now rising from left to right. The battle yell! It made my hair stand up.

Then and for an unmeasurable time thereafter, with the cannon blasts above and those in the field and beyond, with the rip and crackle of rifle fire and the long rising falling cry, it was like a maddening tempest of sound enacted around us in that hollow rock. It canceled thought and every sense but the vision in my transfixed eyes of the battle spread out before me: the bloom of bursting cannon balls in wreaths and tatters of smoke, spurts of flame and silver flashing, figures made dim in the gathering haze, running and falling and thrusting man to man till one or the other went down in death or wheeled away and fled. A white horse rearing shed its rider and standing gigantically upright in the smoke, fell like a tree on a seething cluster of bodies around a pitching battle flag.

There were certain things I later remembered with special trenchancy, though at the time these registered only as stock events of the battle. One was a shot evidently delivered from close range, from a cannon or howitzer that must have been loaded with such as pieces of chain. Its path was straight through a huddle of writhing figures, carrying with it, as seemed to me, limbs and heads and torsos like fragments expelled from a quarry blast. That and one more special thing recalled in the hours after. It was all the fallen shapes in the wake of the battle line, lying at random and motionless in death, or struggling, twisting in final effort to escape death's tightening hand. But these were horrors to me only in the remembering.

It was when I began to notice how the blue line, already broken and gathered in random clusters, was falling back, that something like full clarity returned to me. They were beaten, already in retreat, and now bugles were calling them back. We were winning, routing them, I thought, in a great rush of elation that brought a cry to my lips. Or would have done, except for what suddenly happened.

It was an explosion that made the ground shake and shards of stone from up above rain down in front of my face. I heard Dink's voice. A stone had grazed his forehead, leaving a gash and blood beginning to seep. "Get back," I cried, already stepping back. Then it happened again, and then another time. They were shooting at us. This was my thought, but after that I understood. It was our cannons above us on the hill that they were trying for. "Get back against the wall!" We did, did it in the very instant when came another explosion, successive explosions that sent the chunks raining down again.

"What if that fall on us!" He was looking up at the rock ledge low above our heads.

"We got to get out of here! Quick!"

We lunged in the same instant and out and sharp right through the thicket along the steep hillside. The explosions that followed, though not so near, were jolts that propelled us with all our strength through the ripping undergrowth.

We ran in a sort of blind confusion for what must have been several minutes. Where I, in the lead, stumbled almost falling into a gully we caught ourselves back and abruptly crouched down in what seemed a partial shelter. The cannon shots continued to come, though diminished now from their former jolting force.

"We goan just stay here?" Dink's wide eyes were scanning the woods around us. The battle noise, if a bit more distant, seemed scarcely less than before.

"You want to?"

"Might do better we was far side of this hill."

I thought for a moment. "We better stay off that ridgetop, though. Let's keep on like we are, circle around the end slope."

We went more slowly now, with a needless caution, as if stealth would make us safer. But finally, rounding the end slope of the hill at a place where the trees thinned out, we saw down below a sight that abruptly stopped us.

At the foot of the hill among cedars that half concealed them from view were soldiers, our soldiers, a great number of them. They were just standing there, waiting, it appeared, on something we could not see. Beyond them, at a distance I guessed as perhaps a quarter mile, was the railroad cut that Mr. Hoop had mentioned to me: a deep gash between vertical walls extending some hundreds of yards.

"Reckon what they doing?" Dink murmured.

"I don't know. Let's wait and see." Crouching, we settled ourselves to wait.

The diminished din of the battle continued in my ears, but I had stopped listening to it. Watching those soldiers standing silent in the camouflage of the cedar green down there, I was surer minute by minute that something dramatic was about to happen.

"Look, coming," Dink whispered, raising his hand to point. A step sideways and I could see it too. There were Yankee troops, maybe a whole regiment of them, crossing the railroad at the far end of the cut and wheeling our way in parallel to it. At shoulder arms, without any visible sign of caution. An ambush, then, it was to be! Shifting my stance for clear sight through the trees, I watched them come on, closer and closer, the hot blood mounting in my veins. There was something strange.

Suddenly, "Them's niggers!"

Dink's pitched voice had said it. "Shh," I said, with a glance at his astonished face. A minute more and those black troops would be in easy musket range. But suddenly they stopped, wheeling around in confusion, bringing their rifles violently in hand. It was yet a minute more, however, before I saw the reason. Not that I could actually see, but I knew already the cause of their confusion. Then I could hear it, the high-pitched yell of Confederates charging, moving now into partial view toward the rear of the Yankee column. Just faintly above the Confederate cry I heard what must have been orders screamed out, and saw the column abruptly scatter in the effort to form a line. But that too broke in confusion. Our men in the cedars below us were the reason. Already bursting out of woods, already at full cry, they split to form half of a surging lunette that in moments completed the trap. I remember thinking how perfect it was, how brilliant at every step: the black Yankees caught with their backs to the cut and the long jaw closing in.

If in fact that Yankee regiment added more than a few wild shots to the general din of musket and rifle fire, it was not evident to me. Within moments after the firing began, the disorder among them had lapsed into a chaos of men lunging and scurrying this way and that, falling and sometimes rising again, crying out and upraising arms in surrender that only made them better targets for the Confederate fire. And then came the bayonets. Some fought back with their own for a little space, but not to any visible effect. Disarmed in that battle terror that takes men by the throat, their one choice was blind retreat wherever it might lead. So it was that many of them, wounded and not wounded, with blood-tipped bayonets at their backs, hurled themselves over the edge of the cut to a drop of forty feet. The last one, the one I will never forget, went over with bayonet, rifle and all protruding from his back.

But it came to an end, all at once, it seemed. Dead and wounded black soldiers, with a few Confederates scattered among them, littered the ground for a hundred yards along the edge of the cut. Those on their feet, still a great many, already were being herded at gun point into a column for marching. Last of all I suddenly noticed what some of our men were doing. Moving from fallen body to body, they knelt and stripped the limp black forms of boots and hats and coats. Turning away from the sight of it all, I said uncertainly, "We better go on."

Dink did not look at me, maybe had not heard. He was watching the black column now in motion, the guards strung out on either side with rifles held at ready. Finally he said, "Where we goan go?"

"Other side the railroad. On east. Like Mr. Hoop told us."

"Them Yankee niggers comes from there. Prob'ly be some more of them, one kind or other." He paused. "Else't Confed'rates."

The tone of his voice was strange, new to him. So was his expression, gloomy and sullen as I never had seen it before.

"Don't you want to try to get home?"

"Ain't no way to."

I hesitated. "Dink . . ." But I did not know how to go on. Finally, to break this drawn-out silence between us, I said, "Maybe we could go back to that barn. Just stay there till it's all over."

Dink did not answer.

"I think we can find it. Go on up the railroad past this hill, then back west. Oughtn't to be but a few miles."

"Awright." But that was all he said, and he didn't even look at me. We just stood there. Since last I had noticed, the noise of the battle we had left behind was greatly diminished, indeed had almost stopped. I did not remark on it. At last I said, "Come on," and started away.

Dink followed, but not up close anymore.

$\mathcal{My}$ leading us back westward with the aim of returning to that barn was truly an instance of deserting the frying pan for the fire. In my ignorance I assumed that what I had so far seen was enough to instruct me as to where our safety lay. Supposing the full-scale battle to be now under way all along the established line and having witnessed what appeared to be Confederate success, I took it that a westward course at some distance behind that line would keep us safely clear of the fighting. But in fact the real battle, and that not until mid-day, would begin on the Confederate west flank. Because of overwhelming numbers and superior artillery the Yankee attack met with considerable early success, and it was not long before the Confederate line began to retreat from some of its advance positions. The result, quite before we realized it, was to put Dink and me in real danger of Yankee and also Confederate fire. But this came later in the day.

It is most likely that if we had continued on our way at good speed we could have, in the few hours of grace left

to us, made it safely back to that barn. There, as I calcu-
late, we would have been in a position from which flight
southward to safe territory would have been easy. But we
did not continue at good speed. The lesser reason was a
certain indecision on my part. Quite foolishly, I know,
I was not really much afraid of the clear dangers that
might befall us. It was as if, having escaped that one
close call back there and finding ourselves now alone
and unthreatened in open sun-lit pasture land, we were
somehow exempted from further perils. And there were
the thoughts of my father and now also of my surely desperate mother that came and went in my mind. These
were factors, but the greater cause for our hesitant pace
was Dink.

From the start it was clear that the grisly event back
there by the railroad cut had shocked him deeply—as,
in a way less acute, it had shocked me. But his lagging,
his persistent and sullen silence as we went on, increasingly weighed upon me. I thought of words that might
comfort him, words that to me were resolution enough.
'That's what war is,' I wanted to say. 'Black or white,
they were Yankees.' But every time I looked back at
him, the words would dry up in my mouth. They would
have got no answer.

We went on like this for an hour or more, up hillslopes
through cedar and hardwood thickets, and down and
up again. We passed an empty farmhouse or two and
crossed a pike—the one to Franklin, I guessed. Later,
in a field of sere and broken corn stalks where the
ground was still half frozen I slowed my steps in hopes
of finding a few ears yet intact. Dink slowed too, but not
to look, keeping his distance still. At last, spying an ear,

I stopped and picked it. "Look," I said. "If we can find a few more of these . . ."

In a voice just audible he said, "It ain't no 'count."

I stripped the shuck. He was right, the grains were black with rot. I said, "Anyhow I got those hoe cakes. Mr. Hoop put them in my pocket. You want to eat them?"

"I ain't hongry." His face was a black and sullen mask.

Moving on, I did not try again.

All along I had been hearing, from beyond the ridge just to the north of our passage, only subdued and intermittent sounds of battle. This fact allowed me, in hopeful moments, to suppose that the Yankee army was in retreat, falling back toward the city. In any case I saw no great cause to hurry, and soon, tired and cold as I was, I began to look about us for a place to rest awhile.

This took some time yet, but suddenly, cresting a hillock, I saw in the near distance a small white house and barn near the foot of a high wooded hill. It had the look of desertion: not so much as a chicken came to view. I said, loud enough for Dink to hear, "Looks empty. We could take a little rest there, maybe. Get warmed up some." Then, "We could eat these hoe cakes."

"Awright," he said, murmured. He followed as before, down the slope and on across the field.

The farmer had taken everything with him: stock, tools and, from what I could see through a window, all but his heaviest furniture. The porch door was shut but not locked and for a moment, as if expecting some painful issue, we just stood there in the cold, nearly barren room. A massive table, forgotten fire poker against the rock chimney, a half-burnt stick lying in ashes there. A fire? There might be firewood out in back. The thought passed through my head and was gone.

But I found a way to get almost warm. It was a ragged carpet I found in another room, and I dragged it out and into a corner next to the fireplace. "Come on, Dink. Get under," I said from my crouch, holding the carpet up in readiness for him. But he just stood looking not quite at me, a look I hated to see, that dropped the weight of it down on my spirit again. I searched in my mind for something, words that might call him back. All I could find to say was, "Come on, Dink. Let's get warm."

Though moving slow he crouched down beside me and covered himself with the carpet. Then, for a long time, silence, like echo ringing off the bare walls. Finally, all but bursting out with it, I said, "They were Yankees too, come to take our country away from us. We got to fight back."

The silence again, but this time it was brief. He said, "They was niggers just like me."

Nothing more, nothing to comfort my distress. At last I thought of the hoe cakes in my pocket and fetching them up, all broken, I held out some of the pieces to him. Indifferently he took them and while I ate with sudden hunger merely nibbled at his own. "There'll be a well," I said. "I'll get us some water." This got no response and I let it pass.

In time, in the warmth the carpet furnished, my tired thoughts went adrift. Father came first among them, up there in the line someplace, on a horse and without fear driving the harried Yankees on before him. Then it was my mother. Two days, I had promised, seeing her taut pale face again, her hand on Liza's forehead. For some time the memory racked my thoughts, subsiding only when at last her image lost all distinctness. Sleep at last came down like rescue from my distress.

I do not know whether Dink slept too, but he was awake when I opened my eyes, awake with a different attentive look on his face. There was noise. It was not gunfire, it was voices and thumping of many feet and clatter and rattling. In seconds I was at the window seeing men, ours, a host of them, and horses and cannons and wagons filing past. Then, as by an explosion, the door flew open. There was a tall man, an officer, and several men with rifles coming behind him. Then the officer's voice: "Set up in here. Take those windows." And the men, dividing around him, took place at each front window. Already turning to leave, the officer saw me. "What the hell," he said. "Get out of here, boy. They'll be shooting this way any minute now. Get up that hill back there and on away from here fast."

It was as if I had fallen stupid. I think my mouth fell open.

"Have I got to drag you out?" His voice had risen in anger. Spotting Dink he said, "Him too. Get!"

I think I had a foot already forward when I was not only stopped but riveted in my tracks. The cannon shot had struck so near that the window glasses flashed with orange light. "Goddamnit!" the officer screamed. "Get!" Then, "You men too."

Suddenly I was in motion, running toward the back door and through and out where cries and screams of pain seemed as if suspended in the medium of air. There was somebody behind me and I remember thinking, through that second or two before I reached the backyard gate, that it was Dink. In fact, for some indefinite interval beginning with a stroke of white light inside my skull, this was the last thought I had.

It was quiet around me and I was lying under a cedar tree, alone. No, I was not alone. There was a man lying close by, a dead man with a bloody broken face. For some moments, propped on my elbow now, my brain swimming with the sight of him, I continued to lie there. In the distance it was not quiet: it was POM after POM of cannons and subdued unbroken rip and rattle of musket and rifle fire.

I got to my knees and holding to the tree trunk stood up. Somehow I was in woods near the foot of the hill, and the house was just below me. House? It was not a house any longer: it was smoking sections of upright walls where tips of flame still played, and one surviving sagging piece of a roof. That was when the thought of Dink started into my mind. Scanning, scanning the woods around me I thought of calling his name, and maybe did. But there was the stillness. My gaze leaped back to the ruin below me, and settled there.

I was running, or trying to, staggering down the slope. The backyard gate was there like a memory and where the backdoor had been there was no wall. Beyond was rubble in heaps and scatters and acrid stink of char. I saw a protruding foot. But the foot was bare, white, the toes tinctured with blood. Where Dink and I had sat was no wall now, was a jumble taller than my head of shattered beams and roof boards and rocks from the fallen chimney. Leaning close, dizzily peering into the spaces between, I heard myself calling his name. An answer somewhere? I listened, called again. Then, from under a slanting beam, his dim face appeared. His eyes were looking at me. "Dink," I said. His eyes looked . . . but did not look. It was some long time before I understood that this was a death stare I was facing.

I have only a sketchy recollection of the interval, maybe hours long, that followed this understanding. I had suffered not only the stunning concussion from that cannon shot but also from some object that had struck me somehow on the side of my head. This last I discovered later, feeling the wound with my fingers and then the dried blood on my cheek and neck. So that moment in the stare of Dink's eyes was shock upon shock and for quite a while afterwards partly obscured my clarity of mind. The memories I have retained from that interval are partly of dreams or illusions that still seem perfectly real.

But one thing that surely did happen was my extended effort to reach and extract Dink's body from the rubble. At full strength I might have been able to do it, but in my condition, weak and dizzy, continually losing my balance, the jam of heavy beams defied my best efforts. I remember, as I worked, talking to him as though he were alive, promising rescue and urging him to extend his hand. At a point that marked the conclusion to my efforts I was able, by some accidental contortion, to reach in far enough between the beams so that the tips of my fingers actually touched him. It was some bare part of his body, flesh, and the feel of it in that instant made my fingers recoil.

Where I sat down on a remnant of the floor, and later found myself lying curled-up on my side, was a warm place close to some still-live embers. But though I must have slept, it was not restful sleep. On and on I could not finally escape the sound of Dink's voice from out of the rubble heap. His words were never audible but I seemed to know what he said: he was pleading for help, urging me, accusing me of desertion. I had run away, left him there, content to save myself. At times I tried to answer and strained to get up from the floor. It was not through failure of my will that my body refused to stir.

But there were interludes when the voice was hushed. It was because, off and on, my father was present. I first saw him in the backyard dismounting his horse. The horse was Windward, his claybank gelding, all sleek and proud as on that day when Father rode out for the army. Then Father was at my side, looking down at me, trim and tall in his gray officer's coat with glinting brass on the collar. He had removed his big, plumed hat and stood holding it with both hands lightly against his torso. In a gentle way, almost with a smile, he asked me if I was all right. I felt all right, and I told him so. And I told him about Mother and Liza, how they needed him, and then about Dink lying there in the rubble. Still he looked down with that kindly look that was almost a smile on his face. It would be all right, he said. Soon he would come. Everything would be all right. I asked him if we were winning, and thought he gave a nod. No matter, because the look on his face told me that we were. A handsome face, a soldier's face, with beard gone faintly silver. And yet . . . There began to be something wrong. It had to do with the hat, how he kept holding it with both hands against his torso. Even when I saw that he was gone, distress remained like an object lodged too close against my heart.

He came again, and another time, his bearing just as before. There was something wrong, deeply wrong, hidden beneath that hat.

I heard noises and forcing myself to sit up I saw that it was twilight. Then there were two men standing over me. The one in tattered overalls with a pistol on his belt said, "Come on, boy. Can you stand up?"

I wanted to answer.

"Here. Help him up." They lifted me onto my feet. "Got to get you out of here."

"Dink," I said. Then, "He's under that heap, there."

"He alive?"

It was as though I had to think about it, but I finally shook my head No. "We got to get him out, though. I can't leave him there."

"We'll take care of it." They hustled me out, my feet half dragging, and sat me down at the foot of a tree. "You stay right here."

"Please," I said.

"Just sit tight."

Then they were gone, but not back into the house. I thought about going back, trying again, but the thought soon drifted away in the gathering dusk. There was noise, a rattling wagon drawn by mules, a slumping driver high up on the seat. Passing between the ruined house and me it reached a point where the dusk could no longer hide the nature of its cargo. Stacked a little higher than the tall sideboards, prostrate bodies, ghost-white faces, bare feet in the frigid gloom, jerked and shifted like fretful sleepers transported unawares. At a distance along the foot of the hill the wagon vanished in the dark. Shivering I hugged my knees and hid my face from the cold.

"Boy." A mounted officer looked down at me almost from overhead. "Can you get up?

Whether or not I said it, I thought, "Yes."

Bending from his saddle he reached down. "Give me your hand."

I saw what he meant to do. I said, "I can't. Dink's dead in there. I got to . . ."

"Give me your hand. They'll take care of it. Nothing you can do."

There was his hand. I took it. He gently lifted and settled me astride his horse's cruppers. "Hold on. Put your arms around me." As we turned I saw another wagon passing, another load of the dead.

It was a steep climb, through trampled brush at first, then cedars in a grove. I heard him speak, over his shoulder to me, a gentle voice. "Was that where you lived, in that house?"

"No," I said. Then, trying to raise my voice above the tramping, blowing of the horse, "I . . . we just stopped to rest. It was empty."

"Bad choice," he said. "How'd you come to be here?"

I told him. "Named Jason Moore. Captain. In Cheatham's Corps. Tenth Tennessee, but I couldn't find it."

"Might not even exist anymore. After Franklin."

Beyond the cedars was open ground and light enough to see that the climb grew steeper yet up ahead. He reined in the blowing horse to give it rest for a minute. "Captain Jason Moore," he suddenly said. "I know that name. He did something at Franklin that got him a commendation. A brave man, they say."

Abruptly, with pride, my spirit soared up and for yet a moment or two I could not speak. "He was all right, then," I said. "Wasn't hurt or anything."

"I don't think so. I'm pretty sure not."

Of course. And 'brave' was not the word, not big

enough for my father. The glow was still upon me when we reached the crest of the hill.

There were camp fires spotted along the ridge, and soldiers moving about, and several cannons and wagons that could not have got here by the route we had come. My officer and another held a brief conference about me. Then I was lifted down and escorted to the only tent I saw, a big one with a make-shift table placed in the middle of it. At the back of the tent the soldier, who looked not too much older than I, spread a blanket on the ground. "Lay down there. I'll bring you something in a minute." In much more than a minute he did, a warm bowl of something that looked like porridge and tasted like goober peas. Finally I ate it, all of it, then wrapped myself in the blanket. Still later an older and gentle soldier came and washed the blood from my face and neck and dressed the wound on my head.

I kept on sinking into sleep that never lasted long. Sometimes it would be thoughts of Dink that brought me full awake. Again it would be voices close by, officers in candlelight quietly conversing. I remember mention of Ector's brigade, of a Colonel Shy, of breastworks and emplacements; and especially I remember some discussion about the troops, about men so near exhaustion as these being forced to work through the night.

But work through the night they did. Suddenly waking, I would hear the sound of their labors: hum of voices and orders called out, the clank of shovels, the thump of a felled tree intermitting the constant ring of axes. The number of troops was much greater now than when I had first arrived. Through the open tent flap I could see them along the ridge, in fire and lantern light, figures wielding axe or shovel or at strain emplacing some few new cannons now magically on the scene.

It is ironical that this, the memory of our soldiers constructing those works, should have left me feeling reassured when real sleep finally took me. For in fact, as I was to learn in aftertimes, I had been eye-witness to a most crucial error in the making.

CHAPTER NINE

I was awakened before daylight and, still groggy, led away onto a muddy track that angled down the back slope of the hill. The soldier guiding me, and taking my arm when I staggered, kept talking to me in a strange, youthful voice. "Come from way down in Loosiana," he was saying. "Never don't get cold like here. Rain a lot. Fog come in off the bayoo." I guessed him at maybe fifteen. Fifteen, and fighting. What if, in the day ahead . . . ? I thought of Dink, and stopped. "I've got to go back," I said. He took my arm more firmly and kept me moving on down the muddy track.

He was nevermore going to leave there ever, he said. There were fish a plenty in the bayoo, big cats and reds and bass, and muskrats and beavers and sometimes minks to trap in the swamps around. He paused. "If just the good Lord in his mercy'll lead me safe from this place. My friend Pierre, he was . . ." His voice stopped, for good this time, leaving only the slogging sound our feet made in the track. Down ahead were camp fires.

There were moving figures in the firelight and three wagons with mules standing ready in harness. Men were being led or helped or carried and settled among others on the wagon beds. The rest, listless figures waiting, lay at random on the ground or, propped on an arm or elbow, sat staring into the fire. Wounded men with bloody rags, or none, for bandages. One as he was lifted up exposed a leg like a blood-soaked rope dangling from his knee. But it was another man whose sudden scream came at me like a shot, whose failing voice in the aftermath died out in pleas and curses. The soldier beside me touched my arm, his signal of farewell. I had only a glimpse but his pain-wracked face abides in my memory yet.

A soldier in a Yankee officer's coat stood in front of me. "No more room, boy, squeezed in too tight already. You look like you're able to walk, though, ain't you?" Just as if I had answered yes, he said, "Hold on to one of the wagons. That'll be a help," and turned from me and signaled for the wagons to move on out. I had taken a forward step, myself, when I noticed something that stopped me. It was on my tongue to cry out 'Wait' . . . till I understood that those were dead men lying there in the firelight.

We went on for a long time in the dark and then in first dawn light. There were groans and often bitter cries when the wagons jolted hard, and one man in my own wagon kept on and on calling a woman's name. "Martha, Martha," he would call, as if Martha with her comforting hands was somewhere nearby in the gloom. In the growing light I could see his bloody head, how it rolled and lolled with the pitch and sway of the wagon. A little later I discovered that the man walking beside me who held so tight to the wagon did it because he was blind.

Then suddenly the guns. From beyond the stretch of hills to our left, from all along the extended battle line, I was hearing again the thump and boom as the cannons came to life—intermittent at first, then gathering in crescendo that reached to a constant wavering roar. Next, unmuted by intervening hills, the roar was behind us also, mounting at times to a pitch of sound that made my eardrums quake. It was almost like a moment of actual silence when I was able to hear, faint in the distance, the rattle of musket and rifle fire and, once, a snatch of the shrill fierce yell I recognized now as ours. Above us higher than the hills great drifts of orange-tinted smoke obscured the early sun.

But on we went, the wagons jolting, the pale faces mutely staring or grimacing with pain. There were lulls in the roar of the guns sometimes but never any real relief until (it seemed forever) we rounded a sheltering hill. Then I saw, across a wide green pasture, a house that looked tall and white against the dark grove behind it. A stately house, I thought, standing like peace itself in the sunlit distance.

But I never had been more wrong. There were wagons in a staggered row, litter of rags and bottles and kegs, and everywhere, on the scarred and rutted lawn, on the high steps and crowding the broad veranda, the sick and wounded lay. The dead also, as I was soon to notice, with stark faces gazing at the sky. There were men, some black, and women too, scurrying about, bending down to tend or lift a patient from the ground. And voices everywhere, in mingled groans and pleas for help and tense orders loudly passed from one attendant to another. And more to come, more wounded, which I saw by a sudden backward glance at the field we had just now crossed.

Up to this point I have been rather specific in this account of my experience. Even the harrowing event of Dink's death and its immediate aftermath were not enough to significantly darken my memory of what occurred between that event and my arrival at the field hospital. But at some point in the interval after, there began what I think of as my long nightmare, obscuring or simply obliterating details that I might wish to recall. The cause, I am sure, is easily explained. It is simply that I, at the age of twelve, had by this time experienced more, and worse, than I could bear. And if there was a single event that finally precipitated this condition, it is most likely to have been a sight that confronted me shortly after my arrival. It was what I saw by the side of the house beneath a broken window: a gory pile as high as my waist of severed arms and legs. Even as I stood there in my tracks agape, another, a leg with half a thigh, dropped from the window and bloodily tumbled to the ground at the edge of the pile.

I remember screams from inside that house, audible even within the place of refuge I had discovered for myself. It was at some distance from the house, a small enclosed shed for tools and such, and for a long time, hours at least, I was the lone occupant. There in a corner I sat half-wrapped in sacking against the cold, hearing and not hearing the clamor of voices, the screams, the distant roar, in and out of a sleep like suspension above a dark and echoing abyss. I am virtually certain that I did not at any time enter the house but it seemed to me that I had. Upstairs and down, hearing the screams, I could see myself walking with circumspection among the prostrate bodies, observing the broken, blood-smeared walls where tranquil scenes though much disfigured were still obscurely portrayed.

I was called back by voices. The door stood open and before any person came into view I noticed the change of light and that it was raining. Then one by one three wounded men, two with each a bandaged stump where a leg ought to have been, were bodily brought inside and stretched out on the dirt floor in front of me—close, so close that I could have reached out and touched the bandaged face of one. A tall man wearing glasses was looking down at me.

"You all right, boy?"

I think I nodded. He looked at me for a moment longer, then left and shut the door.

Rain ticked on the board roof. But it was not this or even the smell, the smell of blood I thought, that I was not able to bear. It was the groans of the men, of one and then another or all of them contending. With effort, trying for stealth somehow, I came up onto my feet.

"Boy." One was looking up at me. I held there in my tracks. "Get me some water, please."

My mouth though maybe without a sound spoke my willingness, and choosing places to set my feet I passed across their bodies and out through the door.

I remember still with regret that I never brought him the water. But looking about in that scene of confusion for where a well might be, I was suddenly stopped by the tall man with glasses who had asked if I was all right. He led me to where a cedar tree offered a little shelter and asked his questions. For the first moments, he did . . .

until I managed to make my answers plain enough to hear. These made him pause, then suddenly, "Is your father Jason Moore?" It was a moment that comes back to me like a light suddenly kindled. The man said, "He was here about a week ago, escorting a couple of wounded officers. He looked all right . . . as well as most. You know, my home's just a couple of miles from yours. I'm Dr. Drew Anderson."

He told me to follow him, which I did with such a lightness of step as I never had felt before. My father, here? Just last week? My mind's eye saw him across the field, with a plume and his horse at a canter.

A little later I found myself astraddle the cruppers of a horse, behind a young soldier whose name I wish I could recall. To the pike, then south toward Franklin, Drew Anderson had said. A few miles on and there would be houses with people to take me in. Going fast across the open pasture, at a jolting trot that made me hold tight to the soldier, we approached the bounding line of woods where a passage now came to view. It came in sunlight, all of a sudden, slanting last rays from behind us through a rent in the towering clouds. Over his shoulder, friendly, the soldier said, "Maybe going to clear up. Make it get even colder, though."

I remember that when he said this we were at a point just shy of entering the woods and that only seconds afterward he reined the horse to a sudden stop. He twisted around in the saddle to look behind us, but he didn't say anything, not for a while. Then, "Listen."

But I, even in the clouded state of my mind, was already beginning to hear. Both far away and near, no longer in a wavering roar, there were bursts of heavy cannon and rifle fire. But there was more, sound of a different timbre, faint and intermittent then swelling, ringing like echoes from a chorus somewhere among the hills. Voices . . . but not our voices. And not any longer behind us only but north to our left close by.

"What the hell!" Then he said, "Look!"

Behind us and closer still on our left, from hollows between the hills, dark figures in bobbing jagged streams came pouring into the field—running and falling and staggering up and coming on again. We stared.

"By God, they broke us!"

I wanted to say 'It's them, not us,' but I knew it was not so.

Then a jolt and a blinding orange flash, and instantly we on the headlong horse were deep in the sheltering woods.

I believe that of all my experience through those several days, these were the moments that remain most vivid in my memory—etched as it were in the orange flash of that exploding shell. Although there was fighting yet to come and still more deeds of Confederate valor, I remember, never quite stop remembering, that event as the final obliteration of all our anguished hopes. This and, equally fruitless, a related event I can never manage to fully dismiss as its cause. This was the blunder that night on Shy's Hill to which I was ignorant witness. A crucial blunder it certainly was, that haunts my memory still. Yet I know in my heart it was a blunder that only hastened our ruin.

For some reason, perhaps because of darkness and of haste and confusion in the wake of the long day's pounding by the Yankee juggernaut, those breastworks along the ridge had been wrongly positioned. When up in the afternoon of the following day General Smith's brigade took Colonel Ector's place, it was discovered, too late, that the location of these works, at such a distance back from the brow of the ridgetop, denied the defending force its vision of most of the slope below. So it was that the steep face of the hill was more an advantage to the attackers than the defenders. And so it was that here on this hill later named for the gallant Colonel Shy (of whom I had heard mention that night) began the final decimation of the Confederate army in the West.

The Yankee breakthrough on that hill, leading to others in the pitifully thin line on the Confederate west flank, inspired the panic that quickly spread throughout our army. Even the eastern extension of the line, where our soldiers had been handsomely successful through the whole day, caught the infection of defeat. By half after four in the afternoon the entire army was in rout, fleeing toward the way of escape that the pike to Franklin held out.

I have briefly portrayed what I personally saw of that panic flight of our brave soldiers and I have little taste for elaborating further. But in the interest of making my account as complete as possible I will quote the rather eloquent description afterwards recorded by a Yankee officer named Stone, who evidently had observed the scene from a point of special vantage. He wrote:

"It was more like a scene in a spectacular drama than a real incident in war. The hillside in front, still green, dotted with the boys in blue swarming up the slope; the dark background of high hills beyond; the lowering clouds; the waving flags; the smoke slowly rising through the leafless tree-tops and drifting across the valleys; the wonderful outburst of musketry; the ecstatic cheers; the multitude racing for life down into the valley below—so exciting was it all that the lookers-on instinctively clapped their hands as at a brilliant and successful transformation scene, as indeed it was. For in those few minutes an army was changed into a mob, and the whole structure of the rebellion in the Southwest, with all its possibilities, was utterly overthrown."

CHAPTER TEN

*I*t is difficult for me to be even sequential, much less complete in my account of events following that shell's explosion. But I do remember the first things, the bolting of the horse along that track, my holding tight to the soldier, the rip and slash of low-hanging limbs from the trees on either side. Then figures in our path, men dodging and lurching left and right and furious cries in our wake. Till at last, just where the woods broke off, I felt the jolt and upward heave of the horse brought to a stop. A figure whose twisted face I glimpsed, his body all but hanging, had hold of the horse's bit. Then cries and bodies crowding close and a hand that seized my arm. With force that seemed inhumanly strong it flung me to the ground.

Aware of gathering darkness and falling bitter rain I realized that some time had elapsed. The horse was gone, the horse and my young soldier too, and the scatter of men passing by in the gloom now moved with uncertain steps. One of them halted beside me. He bent, his white face hovering, and took my arm. "Can you get up?" he said. I did, helped by the lift he gave me. "We got to get to the pike," he said, and except for his breathing was silent after that.

The time that intervened before we reached the Franklin Pike is mostly cloudy in my mind. But the things I remember best, all around us in the near distance, were the voices, single voices shouting or many rising together, and rifle fire in fitful bursts and intervals of crescendo. Then suddenly (what I most vividly remember) far to our right beyond a stretch of level field and grove, the flash and boom of a cannon. In moments there were many, repeating and repeating, flash upon flash uniting as one in surges of brilliant light. In fact, on our course southeast toward Brentwood and the pike, we were distant witness to the stand that saved so much of our army. It was Chalmers and Kelley with their hundreds resisting a charge of thousands. I hope it is not mere vainglory in me that in my recollections of that interlude Thermopylae always comes to my mind.

I also remember that wounded soldier who had lifted me onto my feet, and how for some long time in silence he had struggled on beside me. Until at last, without a word, he sank to his knees in the mud. Wanting to help him I reached down but he put my hand away. "You go on, boy."

"If we can just get to the pike," I said. "It oughtn't to be much farther."

He was sitting now, a dark figure with bare slumped head in the bitter falling rain. "Ain't no use. For me it ain't." And finally in a voice hard to hear, "All them months and years from Shiloh . . . come down to nothing but this."

"You'll freeze," I said.

"Go on, boy. Stay to this track, you'll get there."

So, after long standing there in the freezing rain, I went.

The pitch of that battle behind me had still not much subsided when I came on a road where wagons and many soldiers, voiceless men like scarecrows obscurely brought to life, slogged past in the rainy dark. I was set to fall in among them, but I failed. For that was the moment when something like sleep swooped down and shrouded my vision. A hand and then another were holding me upright, and a voice was speaking words that were not clear. Then I could see a shadowy face peering into mine and distantly hear a voice that said, "Make him some room on there."

I lay crowded among kegs and boxes on a jolting wagon bed, by turns awake and not awake to sounds of distant musketry. A cannon too, now and then, a fleeting jolt on the air. Drawing closer, it always seemed, as I drifted into my sheltering sleep again. Until, suddenly awake, I discovered that we had not only stopped but were caught in a seemingly hopeless jam of wagons and caissons and struggling men and mules. But there was movement out ahead. This was the Franklin Pike, and there before me, half obscured in night and rain, the sad remnant of that great army was passing south toward Franklin—south and on into history. But a disciplined army now, a march instead of a flight, a thing that should rightly have struck me with wonder even at the time.

The wonder, however, was something that came to me only in retrospect, from what I was later to learn. Back there on the road I had distantly witnessed a part of what made it so. But an equal part must surely fall to General Stephen Lee. It was he who, on the pike north of Brentwood, alone and in peril of his life, put a stop to the panic, headlong flight of at least a full regiment. A brilliant deed in the absence of which the last of our army must surely have been destroyed. Till this day, just as if I had witnessed it, that scene is alive in my imagination: Lee on his horse in the seething rout of men, his hand with the colors held high. And his voice (in words of a kind not unlikely now to meet with ridicule) upraised with all the strength of his faith, crying out in the tumult, "Rally, men, for God's sake, rally. This is the place for brave men to die."

But wonder or not I well remember the passing of that army: the darkness astir with moving shapes, with voices subdued and rattle of wagons and slog and splash of men's and horses' feet. But all, like the voices, mantled somehow, as if constrained by the distant sound of now-sporadic firing. And soon, even as I drifted off into sleep again, my wagon far back near the end of the train had become a part of it.

Later, in one of those many intervals when my wagon had come to a halt, I was wakened by something strange. At first I thought that it was because of a lightness, a swimming inside my head, and next, the result of a cover spread over me, that I was warmer than before. It was neither of these, it was a sound, a voice singing. No, it was voices in unison, muted voices, from off the road in an aura of light made by a flickering fire. It was a song I knew, "The Yellow Rose of Texas," but not in the way they sang it. The cadence was too slow and sad, but also words were changed. My ear caught some of these and has kept them even till this day. The ones I best remember, in a whole verse, were these:

So now we're going to leave you,
Our hearts are full of woe;
We're going back to Georgia
To see our Uncle Joe.
You may talk about your Beauregard
And sing of General Lee,
But the gallant Hood of Texas
Played hell in Tennessee.

Remembering this song nearly always brings to my mind also a report about General Hood . . . of how, after the rout of his army, he was discovered, by an aide, alone and weeping in his tent.

It was some indeterminable time later when I awakened with my head not only swimming but swimming with an unexpected certainty. By some error of direction we were, though halted for the moment, traveling on the Charlotte Pike, and this very place where we had stopped was where my home was located. I pushed my cover off and with some effort sat up. If it was too dark to see, the house was there. I crawled to the rear of the wagon bed and carefully, holding on, put my feet down. I had to hold on for a moment longer, but then, though uncertainly, I started walking across the road.

"Where you going, boy?" a voice said.

"It's where I live," I said and went on. There was a ditch.

"I can't see nothing," the same voice said.

But I was certain. "It's up there." I stepped into the water and climbed the low bank and, remembering, barely paused to say, "Thank you," and went on. I heard the wagon start up.

That the rail fence was somehow gone seemed unimportant, especially after a few more steps when I felt a road, our driveway under my feet. What did a little trouble me a minute or two after that was my first vague glimpse of the house. In some way I was confused; instead of up to the right of me it was across on my left. But it was there, an inconstant towering pallor in the raining night. I approached, found the walk, then saw the columns framing the dark that shrouded our entryway. But in place of four steps there were three, and on the veranda facing the door I touched a porcelain knob instead of a handle. My confusion came back, increasing. In something like panic I strained at the knob, then knocked, and knocked again,

"What you want? Ain't nobody in there. Ain't nothing in there."

The voice, a deep Negro's voice, came from no certain direction. I had turned around. At the foot of the steps was a silhouette, and then, in light from a lantern abruptly unveiled, a black face looking up at me. It kept on looking. Then, "What you want here, boy?"

I could not answer.

"You live 'round here someplace?"

I had to think. "On the Charlotte Pike," I finally managed.

He kept looking at me, raised the lantern higher. "Ain't that way over yonder toward the river? West of town?" I must have answered, because he said, "What you doing all this way from home?"

"Looking," I murmured. "For my father. I got caught in it."

"In that war, huh." He studied me for a moment longer. "Come on with me," he said.

He kept the lantern light in my path, not far to a darkened cabin. There was dim firelight inside, however, invisible from without by reason of carefully mantled windows. Wide white eyes, those of a large black woman, followed to where I was led and told to sit down by the hearth—a hearth and blackened fieldstone chimney like those in Pompey's cabin. "Set in that heat, there. Dry youse'f." Then, "Get him some cover."

Familiar . . . like Pompey's voice. Shivering, unclear in my head, I leaned into the heat. Then a blanket descending and carefully wrapped by black hands around my shoulders. Like Ella's, Ella's hands. And suddenly, with a throb of bitter pain, Dink was in my mind. There was murmur of voices, speaking of Dink, and accusing eyes fixed on me. But the voice I heard now was gentle. "He need sump'm warm in him. I fix him some broth."

I was aware of being talked to. "Thought you was one them so'diers . . . come to steal. Left me here to guard, but it ain't nothing much I can do. Nor nobody else, neither, time like this. All the world blowed away . . . Don't reckon I know your daddy's name."

"Moore," I faintly said. "Jason Moore." In my mind I saw him, but not on his horse, hatless in the dark and rain. Or like so many others . . . ?

There was rain on the roof and clicking sounds and muffled Negro voices. A bowl was there and broth on a spoon held up and warm to my lips. "This do you good," the woman said, and kept on till the bowl was empty.

This was the last I remembered until, wrapped in covers and stretched out by the fire, I awakened in gray daylight. I was fed again, aware of her face and her husband standing there. "I got to get home," I said.

"Better sleep some more."

I did, for hours, but wakeful intervals came. I remember that in one of these we, the man and I, talked for a little while. "You don't want to get back on that pike now," he said. "Nothing down there now but more Yankees than you ever seen. It's another road back yonder a mile or so'll take you to the Brentwood road. You can go that-a-way. Let you miss the best part of them."

"That's what I'll do," I said, stirring, meaning to sit up.

"Naw. You rest some more. It's a long walk back where you live."

He was still talking when I fell asleep, about his family, the black and the white one too, and what this war had caused. All three of his boys done left him, he said, and gone off God knows where. His one gal too, he reckoned, wouldn't be long about it. And his poor old Master and Misses, that never did have but that one boy and him dead in the war. A slow movement of his head and he lowered his gaze to my face. He was older than I had thought, with wrinkled lids and groove-like creases around his mouth and chin.

It was late in the night, on toward morning, when something awakened me. It was a sound, a steady roar I could not identify. I sat up in darkness that flickered with light not caused by the near-dead fire. I could see the two of them standing, just standing, like shadowy statues that seemed to writhe in the waves of inconstant light. It was behind me, the mantled windows suffused with a throbbing orange glow. I got to my feet.

"Just stay still, boy. Ain't nothing we can do."

"The house!" I suddenly said, and got no answer.

It seemed a long time I stood there, uncertain on my feet, made deaf it seemed by the steady roar like the sound in an empty shell. Then I heard something else, high-pitched voices, cheering. "Yankees," I said, and once more got no answer.

Then they were singing, a song with words I could not hear but a tune familiar to me.

"Having them a party."

A moment more and the woman said, "They liable come in here."

I saw his head turn. "You 'bout right. Get Lulu." He looked at me. "You able, boy?" I nodded and took from his outstretched hands my coat and canvas hood.

Beyond the shadow cast by the cabin the near landscape stood detailed in a flood of tremulous light. But there were cedars to hide us and beyond these a barn. Still we went on in the bitter air, the half-grown girl close beside her mother, till we reached a building, a ruined and empty cabin. "We can hold out here till they gone," he said. "I got these here covers to warm us." They went inside, but I stopped in the door to look back.

Above the cedars a towering flame curled upward toward the sky, its lashing tip dispensing flakes of orange or yellow ash. And the voices singing, that song again, the one familiar to me. I remember recognizing, just ahead of the moment when a sudden fear took hold, that this was their song of praise for the sacred Union. But the fear that seized me came of that flame and the thought of my father's house.

"Better come on inside," the deep voice said.

"I got to get home."

"You sho you able?"

"Yes." Remembering, I added, "I thank you."

"Well." He stepped out through the door. "You see the moon setting over yonder?"

I saw it in a now-clear sky just above the horizon, half of a darkening moon.

"Just head right for it, you'll come on that road leads on to the Brentwood road."

But I paused. "You never told me your name."

"It's Henry Byrne. Same as my Master."

Walking now on frozen ground I headed straight for the setting moon.

CHAPTER ELEVEN

*B*eyond two stretches of open pasture land I climbed a rock fence and came onto a road that was deeply rutted but frozen hard. Though the moon had set I had only a few minutes to walk in the dark. The growing light of first daystreak unfolded ahead of me a landscape of fields and hills that, in my state of mind, appeared not only without life but ominously so. That a rabbit hopped idly across the road ahead and, later, two stray whiteface calves watched me from a leafless orchard, failed to assuage in any degree my crushing sense of a desolation made perfect now and forever. Then soon a farmhouse beside the road, lifeless also except for two chickens scratching in the yard.

But finally there was life, of a kind that made me duck for cover in a plum thicket close by. Just up ahead was the Brentwood road, and approaching, heading east into the sunrise, were mounted Yankees and caissons and wagons in a train. Then voices, uplifted bantering happy voices distinct in the brittle air. From that point on, for a while at least, I kept a sharp eye to either side for possible hiding places.

In the beginning I had imagined that I was now equal to such a walk as lay ahead of me. I was wrong. In less than another mile or so, my feet starting to drag, I saw that I would have to stop somewhere and rest. I did, in sassafras bushes by the road, but soon I was shivering hard in the bitter cold. I was on my feet again when I heard, then saw, another detachment of Yankees coming on, just as before, their voices uplifted in banter. So it was minutes more until I was back on the road again.

I had passed by a couple of deserted houses along the way and when, shortly, my eyes fell on another one I stopped to look it over. It sat well back from the road, convincing in its look of desertion. There was something more. With its two tall columns and narrow porch and balcony overhead, it was all but the image of my own home back on the Charlotte Pike. I set out up the long driveway, my feet somewhat lighter now.

There was no front door. Or rather, no door was visible because, as I soon observed, it lay torn from its hinges flat in the dim hallway. Window lights were broken and ahead of me on the stairs, all the way up to the landing, both banisters were pointlessly ripped away. So it was to either side in the rooms adjoining the hall: chandeliers and mantels rudely stripped from their seatings, walls disfigured with jagged gaps, litter of shattered plaster and white dust everywhere. The owners in their haste to depart had left some furniture, left it to this: all ruined, all flinders now. A riot or drunken party, I remember thinking, and remember even till this day with a rush of bitterness. Standing there, looking about me, I felt a sort of numbness taking hold. I found a piece of carpet and in a corner settled myself to sleep.

It was long but never much of a sleep. Dink kept coming back, and Pompey behind him, blaming me. And Mother, and Liza with her small wan face; and Father, his hat held low against his body now, looking down at me. Our house, too, kept coming back, a blackened ruin now. This went on and on, in and out of sleep. When finally I came clear awake the sun was no longer shining. The solid bank of cloud was the kind that promised sleet or snow.

Back on the road I walked for a while without so much as a glimpse of a living thing. Then just ahead a road joined mine, but not, as I had been expecting, a crossroad that would be the Hillsboro Pike. It led north toward the city, however, the direction I needed to go part way, and so I decided on it.

In fact, as I learned afterwards, this was the Granny White Pike where, in half a mile or less, I would come on the scene of that holding action to whose fury three nights before I had been a distant witness. Now approaching it I was warned, by buzzards reeling and winding in circles against the bank of cloud, before I came in sight of the actual scene.

The first thing was a horse dead by the road, torn by the cluster of squawking buzzards that rose, ungainly, on clashing wings as I drew nearer to them. Then, beyond the half-demolished barricade that blocked the way ahead, the whole of that blasted landscape lay in view. Extending far out in the fields and thickets, everywhere were scorched and broken trees and great holes torn in the ground and wrecks of cannons and caissons and wagons scattered about. Even a house, a skeleton, like blackened bones assembled. And many horses, some dismembered, food for the ravening varmints. Somewhere out there one horse was alive, whose feeble neighing afflicted my ears like pain. That feeling of ruin, of final desolation, came over me again. And soon there was more, imagined or not: the death smell now proclaiming itself against the bitter cold. But not of men, I told myself, who had surely been taken away. I withdrew my gaze too late, however. The thing was there close by in an icy ditch, a mangled naked foot protruding from a blood-black trouser leg.

Already sickening, I turned my back on the scene and started away. There was somebody coming toward me, in a buggy drawn by a mule.

The buggy came creaking and rattling on, the sound of it strangely resonant on the motionless brittle air. But the thing truly strange was to see that the single occupant, shaded under the buggy's swaying canopy, was a woman—a woman in a bonnet and cloak not made of common stuff. A woman not young, either, as I saw when she drew rein and looked down sharply at me. Just for a moment, though, before she lifted her gaze and let it wander, with pauses here and there, across the desolate scene. Her tight lips parted, hung loose for a minute, then set themselves again. She looked at me. In a voice a little impeded at first she said, "What are you doing here, boy?"

Finally, croaking a little, myself, I said, "Trying to get home."

"Where is that?"

"On the Charlotte Pike."

Her eyes, for all their sharpness a little rheumy, blinked. "A long ways. Why are you here?"

Somehow I had to think for a second. "I came to look for my father. Before it started. I got caught . . ."

She waited. Then, "All by yourself?"

I could not answer. Dink, I thought, seeing him in my mind, seeing his shadowed face in the pile of rubble.

"Who are you?"

Even this came hard to my tongue. "Steven Moore. My father is Jason Moore." 'Is?' It had to be 'is.'

"I know of him. I live on White Bridge Road. I am Mrs. Elizabeth Wentworth." Then, "Get up here with me."

I did, with a little effort, her gloved hand on my arm. Then, without a word, she reached back to the seat behind and taking one of the blankets there draped it over my shoulders. She said, "When did you eat last?"

I had to think. "Yesterday."

Again she reached back and from a paper bag took a pone of cornbread. "Eat this." She watched me take a bite, then took up the harness lines. "We will have to go another route." Backing the mule, commanding him in a testy voice, she got us turned and on our way at last.

"He is not much of a mule," she said. "I had to borrow him. They took all our horses long ago. Along with nearly everything else." Gazing straight ahead, she was silent for a time. I noticed how her mouth was set, her lips tightly pinched. The sagging brim of her bonnet shaded eyes that had, even so, a visible glint of anger. She said, "I cannot believe that God will ever forgive them for what they have done. Not all of them, perhaps.

General Buell was one. A gentleman. Do you remember him, boy? that he resigned from the Union army? Because he had not known that he was sent here to destroy civilization."

Not remembering, I nodded anyway, my eyes now directed straight ahead where the Brentwood road was in sight. It was only here that uncertainly a question came into my mind. It was answered before I could ask it.

"I am going to take you home, but not yet. I am like you, looking for somebody. For my son. I think it is possible he may be in a field hospital somewhere nearby. I have looked everywhere else . . . I heard a rumor . . ." Her voice, grown dim, now faded out entirely. But only moments later she seized a riding crop at her side and laid it smartly across the mule's rump.

At the junction she drew rein, but not for the purpose of scanning the road both ways, as I surely did. She reached under her cloak and took a piece of paper from a leather bag. What really caught my eye, however, was the polished handle of a pistol protruding from the bag. I remember wondering if, given the occasion, she would be willing, and able, to use it. I thought that most likely she would.

For a few moments she studied the paper, where a rude map was faintly drawn in ink. She put it away and whacked the mule and headed us left toward Brentwood. If there was danger out on that road, nothing whatever in her face betrayed a consciousness of it.

In fact there was danger, or at least the quite alarming appearance of it. We had been only a few minutes on the road when it met us in the shape of four Yankee soldiers approaching on foot. They stopped to watch us draw near, spaced across the road in a manner sure to block our passage. Yet on we came, the face at my side gazing ahead as though at the distant horizon. "What're we going to do?" I said, murmured.

"Sit still."

Yet some steps from the soldier directly ahead she reined the mule to a stop. The soldier off to our left, a wide grin on his face, called out, "What you stop for, Miss High Lady? That fine mule get tired?"

"Come here, young man."

A second or two went by. The soldier's grin was still there, but uncertainly so.

"I want directions," she loudly said. "Come here where I can talk to you."

One of the soldiers guffawed. Our soldier, who had stopped grinning, moved a little, half a step, and halted.

"Come nearer, please."

He did, several paces more, and stopped again. It was a young face, with a faintly puzzled expression.

"I want to know the way to a field hospital. It's somewhere close by."

For a moment the soldier looked as if he did not understand the language. Finally, "I don't know, lady. Back over there, someplace." He pointed behind him with his thumb.

"Thank you. I appreciate your courtesy." She whacked the mule and we passed among them looking straight ahead. There were cat calls in our wake but that was all. Without looking at me she said, "Northerners. It was better this time, though. It was a close thing, back there on the Hillsboro Pike."

Later, warm in my blanket, drowsing off and on, I

was suddenly conscious that we had stopped. On our left where her gaze was fastened there was a road. "It must be this," she said and starting the mule, turned in. Something came in my head. It must have been here, that night when I left the wounded soldier and found myself on the wagon. Here or farther along, I could not remember. But on we went, the buggy springing and creaking over the frozen ruts, I scanning the road ahead in search of the fallen soldier. There was nothing. At last there were woods we were passing through, and beyond, in my memory all of a sudden, the jolt and blinding orange flash of that ultimate cannon shot.

But stillness prevailed where that had been, and beyond in the distance across the field the house came into view. "I was here before," I said.

"Were you?" Then, "Looking for your father."

"They sent me here. Dr. Anderson, that I met, knows Father. He said he saw him not long ago. He said he was all right."

"Anderson," she said. "That's good, he may still be here. They do that, keep the old staff on, under command."

There were many wagons, some with canvas awnings, parked on the lawn whose paling fence was all but completely demolished. The movement I had seen from the distance was soldiers with stretchers descending the steps, bearing wounded men to the covered wagons. Clearly the number of wounded here was greatly diminished now, for I saw not one where many before had lain on the cold wet ground. A Yankee soldier with a rifle stepped up to where we had halted.

"What you want here, lady? This ain't no place for you to be."

Barely glancing at him, the lady looked straight out over his head. "I want to see your commander."

It was a tight sour little face that looked up at her. It said, "He's busy. You better take this contraption on back where you come from." I was suddenly wrung with a hatred for him.

"I have to see him." Still looking straight out over his head she moved and started down from the buggy. But he was there, close up, his rifle lifted crossways almost in her face. "You get back in there and out of here," he said.

"What does she want?" It was a voice calling from on the veranda, a Yankee officer's voice.

"Wants to see Colonel Brady. I told her she couldn't."

From his place on the veranda the officer seemed to study us for a moment. He descended the steps and approaching stood with his face upturned. It wore a neutral expression, not unpleasant. "What is it you want, lady? I guess I know. You're not the first one."

"My son. Thomas Wentworth. He is an officer."

The Yankee stood faintly nodding his head for a second. "I guess I can find out. But that's the best you can look for."

"Please." Then, as he was turning away, she said, "Wait. Is Dr. Anderson still here? He is one of our people."

The Yankee officer nodded again but this time it meant yes. "Stay here," he said and turning away soon disappeared into the house.

Those were a tense few minutes in the buggy—agonizing for her, I knew, knew by her silence and by the way her riveted gaze held fast on that entrance door. Two men and then two more with loaded stretchers came out and down the steps and on to the wagon nearest. This was repeated and after that with the crack of a whip the wagon moved out. A man in a dark-stained, spattered shirt was coming toward us.

I knew him first by his glasses and then recalled his sallow face. But Mrs. Wentworth was between us, half hiding me from his view. Looking up at her he said, "Mrs. Wentworth, isn't it? I'm Drew Anderson." Then, in a voice that might have said it times and times before, "I'm sorry. He's not here. We have no record of him." He quickly added, "Unless you have reason to think . . . He's probably still with the army."

She turned her face away, barely audible words of thanks drifting from her lips. It was then, because of her movement, that Dr. Anderson had got a clear look at me. His eyebrows lifted. "Boy," he said, "your father's in there."

Why it was that I had not entertained this as even a possibility is hard now to understand. I can only suppose that until this moment, in spite of old wounds I knew him to have suffered, he had always come to my mind in all his strength, standing looking down at me or high on a cantering horse. I think my mouth hung open, a question on my tongue. Dr. Anderson was looking at me, hesitating. Mrs. Wentworth's sad eyes, too, came to rest on my face.

"I'm sorry to tell you . . . he has lost his eyesight. And has another wound besides." He paused. "But I think he may, in time, recover some sight in one of his eyes. There's reason to hope. So don't give up."

There were voices all around, a shout or two, the rattling of a wagon. I finally said, managed to say in a voice that could be heard, "Can I go see him?"

His eyes through the glass of his spectacles kept on

regarding me. I saw him blink, and blink again. "Wait here," he said, and turned away.

The stretcher bearers came and went, back and forth to the wagons. A sifting rain had begun to fall, a whisper on the canopy overhead. I was shivering now, and Mrs. Wentworth's hand was on my arm. Very softly she said, "Blind men learn to see in another way. Besides, he may recover . . . with God's help. Pray for him." Seeing her tears, I turned my head aside and shut my eyes. Pray, I thought, I would try to pray. But the words that came seemed feeble as wraiths and vanished short of my tongue.

I think it was a long time before I felt something, a sort of bump, and opened my eyes to see a Yankee soldier taking our mule from between the buggy shafts. Standing by was another, bigger mule, held by another soldier. I watched with a kind of mute surprise as the two soldiers put our mule's harness on the other mule and backed him in between the shafts. They finished without a word, and then were gone. It was this that had kept me from noticing the figures descending the steps.

There, supported by helping hands on either side, was the man who was my father: my father with his head drooped down and snow-white bandage tied across his face. Not so, I thought and almost said on the impulse of a moment. Then it was gone, displaced by a burning blinding rush of tears into my eyes. So it was that I watched him come on, obscurely near and nearer, a figure swimming as it were in the hot flood of my tears.

"Get down and help him," the voice beside me murmured.

Instantly I did, jumped to the ground and circling the buggy stood there in his path. One of his helpers—Dr.

Anderson, it was—said to him, "Here's somebody to greet you."

I stood in arm's reach of where he had stopped, but my voice had got hung in my throat. Lifting his hand, expectant, my father said, "Who is it?"

I tried to speak, and failed. It was answer enough that after a second I put my hand in his. "Steven," he said. He seized me and held me tight and long against his body. At last, in a voice not much above a whisper in my ear, he said, "They have beaten us, Steven."

CHAPTER TWELVE

*M*rs. Wentworth was not mistaken when she had remarked that there were at least some gentlemen in the Yankee army. She had named General Buell, and now, by reason of his kindness, she, and all of us, had Colonel Brady's name to remember. It was not only because of the pass, sealed and signed by him at Dr. Anderson's urging. The mule, a good one in place of ours, was the Colonel's own idea and gift. It was, in fact, a gift that very likely saved us from fatal consequences.

I need give no very detailed description of that long ride, continuing into the night, before we met with the brief but harrowing ordeal in store for us. Until then, in spite of challenges along the way, answered by that pass from Colonel Brady, we had kept a slow but fairly steady pace. There was rain turning to sleet at times, and intervals when depths of mud challenged the mule's best efforts. But the greater cause of our slow progress was Father, because of his pain. This second wound, as I had discovered, was somewhere about his groin, and it was not more than an hour from our setting out before I noticed dark spots that were blood on the blanket wrapped around him. "It's only a little," he faintly said. "Go on."

In the beginning, of course, he had asked the inevitable questions (which I had answered only in part) but after that the silence he kept went practically unbroken. There were times, when the buggy lurched hard, in which I would see through the dark tangle of beard the flash of his set white teeth, and hear the faint unwilling rush of breath that issued between them. From my forward seat, half-turned, I would watch and watch him. Did he sleep sometimes, upright? The bandage made it hard to tell. And hard also to tell, in certain moments when clarity betrayed me, that this was not some suffering stranger mistaken for my father.

At a junction just before dark set in, Mrs. Wentworth halted the mule. In a tired and vaguely doubtful voice she said, "I am sure this is the road." Turning toward me her haggard face in the last dim wash of daylight, she added, "I am almost sure." Seeing I had no answer, she paused. Then twisting to see behind her she said, "Are you all right, Mr. Moore? It should not be too much longer."

My father moved, lifted his hand. In a strained voice somehow made courteous he said, "I am quite all right, thank you, ma'm."

Mainly these last details linger in my memory because, for whatever reason, they stand as a sort of preface to the event I have anticipated. It could not have been more than a minute after we made our left turn into the road that shadowy figures, two before and one beside us, appeared. Yankees, they were, in uniform, one with a musket or rifle pointed directly at us. Another had our mule by the bit and I think it was his voice, full of menace, that said, "You rebs get the hell down out of that thing. Right now! . . . Now, goddamnit!"

Reflecting back on that paralyzing moment it comes to me that Mrs. Wentworth, by some thread of pure steel in her nature, was not afflicted as I was. I seem to remember noticing, in the first instant and flare of my alarm, her hand slide under a fold of her dress and the pistol obscurely exposed. I even seem to remember her thumb get set on the hammer, and then, what is certain in my memory, an ugly high-pitched voice behind me and hands reaching in, closing on my father. That instant is perfectly clear, as is the surge of rage and hate that made me cry out and throw myself at the man. Then a blow and a thrust that sent me backwards into Mrs. Wentworth's arms, and angry voices and jolting of the buggy—all part of a blind confusion that ended with the pistol in my hand.

I only know that I rammed the pistol straight into that Yankee's face and pulled the trigger and saw him in the flash and smoke catapulted backwards into the dark. An interval followed, a startling quiet, for maybe a second or two. Then another flash, from that musket out there, and the hiss of the ball that passed and tipped my ear. There came a jolt, the buggy lurching forward, and Mrs. Wentworth, whip in hand, lashing the frightened mule. There were hands on the moving buggy, and just for a second, close up to the clutching hands, a face that vanished suddenly by a slash of the lady's whip.

There were shouts, cursing behind us, and a shot that passing close over our heads tore through the canopy. But the mule was headlong running now, the buggy pitching, the road ahead just visible in the lingering stain of twilight.

I can only think, as Mrs. Wentworth said and repeated more than once, that our coming safely through those moments was surely the work of God's hand. Marauders, she said, bent on plunder, and murder too, when it suited. I thought of those hands reaching, seizing Father's arm, and saw in imagination his body lie there bleeding on the ground. That Yankee's face in the pistol flash. He was dead, I had killed a man. But that was God's will too, I thought, His vengeance by my hand. Even so the memory troubled my rest for weeks and months to come.

After that first minute or two there was no indication of pursuit, and a little later, though watchful still, we had to stop for Father's sake. It was his bleeding, that lurching headlong run had made it worse. I remember the ripping sound in the dark, Mrs. Wentworth tearing a piece from her skirt for bandage. "Use this," she quietly said.

And Father, "I thank you, ma'm."

Our next stop, after a long, a plodding time, awakened me from still another interval of sleep. I saw a house, one window dimly lit, that I thought at first was ours. But she said, "This is my home. We will have to stay here tonight. It is necessary." Her strained and feeble voice said why.

So we did, though much against my will. In fact, once we had managed, with the help of the two aged female servants, to get Father into the house, I was near collapse, myself. Early in the morning, at first daylight we would go. But thinking this was the final thing I remember from that night.

Mrs. Wentworth was to become a dear friend in the years ahead, and one of the very few people whom I have most admired. She had been a widow for some years, and after her son went off to the army had only her infirm maiden sister for company in the house. Like so many others, like my mother, she had no choice but to let her fields grow up in weeds and brush. Except for proceeds from the sale of farm and household items (her house now was almost bare of any but the rudest furniture) a garden was her principal means of sustenance. Along with some help from the two old Negro servants, she, at the age of nearly fifty, worked it and did the canning with her own hands. I used to notice her hands, that must in the past have been silky smooth, how they were callused and without grace like those of a laboring man. But with all her trials she was a friend who was never absent when needed. I remember rejoicing when it was reported that her son, apparently in decent health, had only been taken prisoner. And rejoicing again, still more, when after the war was over he came home.

Here, near the end of my story, I will pass over many of the sad details that are easily imagined. On the morning after that night, because my father was still unfit to be moved, I took the mule and buggy (along with that pass, since the mule was Union branded) and set out for home. Although I was not stopped, it was, considering everything, a journey whose end I dreaded the more as I came nearer and nearer. Blind, I had to tell her, and learn the fate of Liza. And Pompey . . . what would I say? The house itself came last to mind, called up by the thought of that one in flames back there on the Franklin Pike.

But the house was standing as ever, though desolate in rain. I had thought to say it all in some gentle way, but there in the house, in the first rush of my mother's tears, the words would not be stayed. And standing behind her was Ella whose cry, "My boy, my little boy," came in a plaintive rising wail that echoed through the house. But I remember just as well my moment of sudden gratitude that followed. Liza was there, on her feet, her pale bewildered face gaping up at me.

Three days later, in the buggy as before, we brought my father home. Because of the stairs we settled him in the parlor, on the bed that Pompey and I carried down from his old room. It was like a sort of beginning, a beginning without promise in a house where, for weeks to come, a guarded stillness seemed to muffle the sounds of our daily life. For my father was now a silent man. Except in speaking briefly of practical matters or, in his courteous way, answering simple questions, his voice was the rarest of all sounds in the house. Only once in those weeks do I remember hearing him ask a different kind of question. My mother was in the room and, as I think he believed, nobody else. He said, "Is there any news of the army?"

My mother hesitated. "They have crossed the Tennessee River. General Forrest has held their army back. They are not pursuing us anymore." No other word was said.

Of course the war was not yet over. In Virginia the brilliant Lee, against all reasonable odds, continued to win successive and astonishing victories. But without support in the West anymore his days clearly were numbered. My father knew this. It showed in his responses, the slow and tentative nodding of his head when, in elation, I brought him the news of another great battle won. His gloom enveloped him like a cloud that never would lift again.

But it did at last, to an extent, and in spite of that still-troublesome wound in his groin he began attending as best he could to daily matters again. He had been fairly comfortable on his feet for only a few days when, one balmy afternoon, he went outside and walked for a while with no guidance but a cane. This, when the weather permitted, soon became his habit. I would watch him go his round, touching things as he passed, stopping sometimes with his hand on a tree or a gate or the garden fence. In time his range increased, as far as the barn, which he would enter, and across to the orchard where he seemed to be counting the trees by touch. At last he was ranging as far as Pompey's cabin, and one day when I followed without his knowledge I overheard a sentence or two in what he was saying to Pompey. Those words came as a shock. Not that the chance of losing our home was entirely news to me. But this, the naming of money in such an amount, cast a frightening light on the matter. Later, by Mother, I was reassured, but the thought had got stuck in my mind.

In April there were two events that I am not likely to forget. The much greater one, of course, was the surrender of Lee at Appomattox. It was a time of deep sadness for us, and not a little anxiety as to what might follow after. And yet, for all that, we could not but feel a sense of release from the weight of those four long years. I know that my father especially felt this and I have always looked on it as partly the cause of what happened not too much later. On a bright afternoon near the end of the month, returning from another of his blind walks, he stopped and went on standing there in the open back porch door. But it was the expression on his face, a pleasant and vaguely puzzled look, that so sharply caught our attention. "I saw something," he said. "I saw it as plain as day, just for a moment. That blooming azalea in the yard."

It took a while yet and never was perfect again, but vision came back in his left eye. An act of God, my mother said, and certainly it was a great blessing for us all. And this was so not only because we loved him. When, in less than a year, our home was taken from us, it enabled him to get a job in a mercantile house in the city. For that was where we were forced to live: in a city still ruled by the Union army, whose soldiers along with unruly Negroes mocked us in the streets. My father despised it then and continued to do so throughout the six years left before he died. They were years of bad health, for the wound in his groin, refusing to heal, was an almost constant source of pain. (That it had deprived him of his manhood may go without saying.) He also suffered from spells of blackest bitterness, most clearly manifested in the practically unbroken silences that accompanied them. To any suggestion that he take the oath of loyalty to the *sacred* Union, he responded always with visible contempt.

Pompey came to visit us once in a while. There had been a time, after I had told him all my story, when I could not meet him eye to eye and tried to stay clear of his presence. But I came to believe that he never had blamed me, not even in those first moments. He was there when we buried my father, a mourner with genuine tears, and continued to keep his friendship with us through all the years till his death. We would sit down together and talk of old times and wish them back to life. He was an old man then and, I suppose, no longer representative of very many other former slaves. But his feelings were real. I feel sure he went down to his grave still yearning for that old vanished world.

In recent years I have again walked over that battle-field, looking for and sometimes finding landmarks I remember. After a little searching I did find, deep in weeds and brush, remnants of the house where Dink had met his end. I looked for graves but did not find any. I climbed Shy's Hill, a long way up, and again without result tried to locate the spot where, from in the tent, I had unknowingly witnessed "the great mistake." I always think of it this way. And looking out from the hill-top over the green field and the ridge of hills beyond, I again remembered Mrs. Wentworth, in the buggy that cold day, saying that she could not believe God would ever forgive them. They might have been my father's words. Or my own words, even now, though thirty-five years have passed.

ACKNOWLEDGMENTS

For details of the battle, I am much indebted to Stanley F. Horn's *The Decisive Battle of Nashville* (Louisiana State University Press, Baton Rouge, 1956).

———

The back jacket quotation from Flannery O'Connor is taken from a letter of July 13, 1963 to Viking Press editor Denver Lindley, and is reprinted with the kind permission of Penguin USA.